PRIZE AND PREJUDICE

BOOK 2: ANGIE PROUTY NANTUCKET COZY MYSTERY SERIES

MIRANDA SWEET

HIDDEN KEY PUBLISHING

Copyright © 2017 by Hidden Key Publishing, Inc

All rights reserved.

No part of this book may be reproduced in any form or by any electronic or mechanical means, including information storage and retrieval systems, without written permission from the author, except for the use of brief quotations in a book review.

PRIZE AND PREJUDICE is a work of fiction. Names, characters, places, and incidents are products of the creator's imagination or used fictitiously. Any resemblance to actual events, locales, or persons, living or dead, is entirely coincidental.

"For thirty years," he said, "I've sailed the seas and seen good and bad, better and worse, fair weather and foul, provisions running out, knives going, and what not. Well, now I tell you, I never seen good come o' goodness yet. Him as strikes first is my fancy; dead men don't bite; them's my views—amen, so be it."

— Robert Louis Stevenson, Treasure Island

Chapter 1

THE TREASURE HUNT

Weekends after Thanksgiving on Nantucket had always been a little nuts, honestly. Not as busy as they were on the mainland, perhaps, but not without their share of eager crowds and overwhelmed shopkeepers, either. Shoppers came over on the ferries and wandered the well-decorated island in a holiday mood. Light poles were wrapped with tinsel. Parking meters received big red bows. Lit Christmas trees floated in rowboats in the water. A giant wreath was attached to the Brant Point Lighthouse. Carols echoed from every shop as the tourists flowed through the town, buying caramels and ornaments and antiques, waking up to the smell of maple syrup and pomegranate waffles at the B&Bs, and listening to Santa's belly-laugh as he and Mrs. Claus took an honorary stroll at the Nantucket Hotel.

But weekdays?

Weekdays were supposed to be dead so that Angie would have time to deal with all the book orders that she needed to have shipped ASAP from her bookstore, Pastries & Page-Turners, in time for Christmas.

Instead, on a Tuesday, the bookstore was positively packed with shoppers.

"Oh, Aunt Margery," she said. "I almost resent the fact that Walter came up with such a brilliant idea for whipping up business on the island during the holiday season. Couldn't he have waited until after Christmas?"

"You don't mean that," Aunt Margery said.

Angie sighed. She didn't, really she didn't. She was so far into the black at this point that there was no question that she and Aunt Margery would be able to afford a vacation to the Mediterranean in January.

"You're right." She would suck it up and, in fact, feel grateful for the business. It wasn't just Pastries & Page-Turners that Walter's treasure hunt idea was benefitting, but the whole island.

Angie had moved the register off the tall side counter and onto an antique desk so that Aunt Margery, who was really her great-aunt, could check out customers without having to stand on her feet all day long. Angie was handling customer requests and other emergency issues. The café counter was being managed by Angie's first non-relative employee, a young woman named Janet Hennery who made decent espresso drinks without getting flustered, even if the line almost stretched out the door.

The front door jingled, and Angie crossed her fingers that it was from a customer leaving—not a new one coming in.

"Hello?"

But the voice was coming from the back of the shop, not the front. Angie sidled through the customers, excusing herself as she went, and came face to face with Mickey Jerritt, who was holding a large flat white paperboard box.

"Hello!" He exclaimed when he saw her. "Backup pastry delivery, courtesy of my sister, who sends her regrets as she cannot get away from the shop at the moment."

"You still have extra pastries?" Angie asked incredulously. Mikey and his twin sister, Josephine, were the owners of the nearby Nantucket Bakery, a popular local destination.

"I think the general idea was that after I delivered a bunch of them to you, we wouldn't," Mickey said. "And then we could close up."

"I'll take 'em," Angie announced without hesitation.

"Nothing fancy, just cupcakes with frosting and sprinkles."

"I could sell sugar cookies dusted with green sugar at this point. Everyone seems to be starving tonight!"

She looked for a path through the crowd toward the café counter that would be wide enough to accommodate the enormous box, but there wasn't one. Mickey grasped the situation and hoisted the box overhead, then said loudly, "Excuse me! Sweets coming through!"

People laughed, but they scooted out of his way. Angie followed in his wake and held the box while he unloaded the cupcakes into the display case.

"White with red jimmies is for red velvet. Red with white jimmies is for white peppermint with pomegranate jam. Green with black jimmies is for chocolate peppermint with mint crème. White with green jimmies is for rosemary mint."

"Rosemary mint?"

"Everyone went nuts for them at the bakery this morning, so I thought I'd try them out on you. White with the little blue snowflakes is blueberry crunch. The ones with the tan frosting with tiny marshmallows are burnt marshmallow and bourbon. Chocolate frosting with tiny marshmallows is hot chocolate, and the ones with the red and green candied fruit on the gold-dusted frosting is fruitcake."

Angie laughed. "Fruitcake! I don't think anyone will buy those."

"They're not real fruitcake. Just the best rum-soaked cupcakes with candied fruit that you'll ever eat. Just because you can use some fruitcakes to beat up burglars doesn't mean that they're all bad. *Mine* are great."

"I'm sure. I'll save one to split with Aunt Margery and let you know how it tastes."

He grinned at her, then hefted the empty box back overhead.

"Thanks, Mickey," she said. "Janet? Did you catch all that?"

The espresso machine screeched as Janet pulled a double shot. "I think so!" she shouted over the noise.

Angie sighed in relief, then worked her way through the crowd toward a waving customer who wanted to know if she had any books on the lost Monet of Nantucket. About a dozen other customers hushed as they heard the question.

If she'd *had* such a book, then there would have been a stampede for it.

She said, "I'm sorry, nobody has written one. Maybe after the painting is found!"

Several people laughed.

"And I'm afraid we're completely out of books on Monet at the moment, although we have an entire section on the history of the island..."

She led them toward the correct shelves, which were already surrounded by treasure hunters.

Walter Snuock had inherited half the island of Nantucket after his father's death in July. His father had been about to raise the rents on all his properties in order to bring them in line with market value. Walter was trying a different method of achieving prosperity by hosting a treasure hunt to find a lost painting, a genuine Monet, that had disappeared almost a hundred years ago.

There was a hundred-thousand-dollar reward for the painting, which was estimated to be worth over one and a half million dollars. None of the residents of Nantucket or their families or employees could win the reward—it had to be a tourist. If the painting was found, it would be put on public display at the Chamber of Commerce.

The result was that the whole island had gone completely mad every day of the week so far.

She simultaneously wanted to hug Walter and shake him.

But he had been making himself scarce on the mainland lately. He had stirred the pot, then left everyone else behind to deal with the rolling boil. He was a lawyer in Manhattan, and he had several cases to wrap up before he could spend more time on the island.

And with her.

∼

At eleven o'clock, Angie closed the doors and locked up. Her eyes were burning and her legs ached. She should have gone straight to the boxes she was packing and worked on them, but instead she found a comfortable overstuffed chair in the café area and sat down.

A cappuccino appeared in front of her. Or at least, something resembling a cappuccino. She could tell just by looking at it that there wasn't enough foam mixed in with the milk and espresso, but it was an improvement over Janet's early attempts.

Angie smiled up at Janet. "Thank you. Why don't you finish closing the coffee bar and take off for home?"

"I think I will. What a day. I hope they find that picture soon, don't you? Or at least that people get bored with coming over here to hunt for it. If it were something you could find in a single afternoon, someone would have found it already. I actually had someone ask me if he could start pulling up floorboards to look!"

Aunt Margery claimed the chair next to Angie's. "I had someone try to pull the drawers out of the desk...while I was sitting at it!"

The three of them shook their heads. The treasure hunt seemed to be giving the normally-polite tourists justification for acting like children.

A soft *"meow?"* echoed from the back of the shop. Angie turned around and spotted Captain Parfait, the store kitty. He was a large tortoiseshell cat with a scar over one eye, a ragged ear, and a limp. Angie had adopted him within a week of opening the bookstore, and fortunately, he seemed content with his limited territory. Although he did have a tendency to shred anything that looked even vaguely mouselike that he could get his paws on.

Angie clucked her tongue and scratched her knee, which was her way of inviting Captain Parfait to climb up on her lap. He did so, headbutting her chin before settling down to be petted.

Janet reached over, gave Captain Parfait a scratch behind the ears, then headed back to the café area.

"What do you have left to do?" Aunt Margery asked.

"Everything. I wasn't able to get to a single thing."

"Why don't you go home and get some sleep, then come in early?"

Aunt Margery was infamous for staying up late and sleeping in. Some days, she wouldn't appear until after noon. Not that Angie could complain. She was lucky to have Aunt Margery's cool head as well as her expertise at reading people. And, after the events of last July, she was lucky to have Aunt Margery's affection and friendship.

Angie's first murder case had nearly caused a family tragedy, as Aunt Margery and Angie found themselves embroiled in the mystery.

But that was over now.

No more murders. She just didn't have time for them.

"I can't," she told her great-aunt. "I have too much to do, and I don't want you carrying all those heavy boxes of books around."

"I can carry 'em," Janet announced.

"You're going *home*," Angie said. "Remember?"

Janet laughed. "Actually, I'm going out with some friends."

"Then that's even more important." Angie dug her fingers into Captain Parfait's fur and gave him deep, massage-like scratches. He stretched out all four paws until his toes were splayed. He purred loudly.

Then, after a few seconds, he hopped down and began to prowl around the shop. He could only take so much spoiling before he had to get away and pretend that he was the fierce and untamed hunter of his youth.

Angie rose from her chair and tried to shake off the feeling that she was at least a hundred years old. Maybe the cappuccino would help. She took an experimental sip and gave Janet a thumbs-up. Not bad. Then she carried her cup into the back office, which also served as the stock room, and booted up the computer.

The priority tonight, she decided, would be to get the boxes of books packed and ready for the delivery driver to pick them up in the morning. The rest of her tasks would just have to wait. She would keep her fingers crossed that someone would find the painting soon. Of course, right after the painting was found, the island would be even *more* crowded as people came to see it, but at least there would be an end in sight.

She checked over her orders, printed out the receipts, and started pulling books out of boxes. She stacked some books on her order table and the rest on a sheet on the floor, placing receipts on top of the completed piles. She'd be surprised if she was out of the store before midnight.

Putting it all in order was deeply satisfying, and she found herself whistling happily as she worked.

Suddenly she came upon the slip for Reed Edgerton, who was ordering, not bestsellers or thrillers or cozy mysteries, but books on the subject of Nantucket. She chuckled. He was an art professor at Harvard who taught Eighteenth and Nineteenth century art history. His favorite painter was J.M.W. Turner, a unique Cockney artist who had worked in the Nineteenth century. Turner's work wasn't entirely to Angie's tastes, but she couldn't seem to stop staring at it, either. She had stopped to examine one of his paintings at the Boston Museum of Fine Arts and found she couldn't look away.

From behind her, someone had said, "Eerie, isn't it?"

She had almost jumped a mile. "Yes, actually, although I'm not quite sure why."

She found herself facing a shorter man with broad shoulders, light-brown skin, and a beard speckled with white. His hair had receded like the tides and left a gray-pebbled bald spot behind. He smiled.

"You haven't read the title yet, have you?"

She hadn't. She leaned forward and read the brass plate at the bottom of the large oil painting. It read, *Slave Ship (Slavers Throwing overboard the Dead and Dying—Typhoon coming on), 1840*.

She looked at the painting again and gasped. Amidst the beautiful colors and atmosphere of the painting were what she had assumed were fish or birds at first glance—hands reaching out of the water, and links from several enormous iron chains.

"The painting has been carefully composed so that it strikes almost every viewer in the same manner," the man said. "The sunlight in the middle of the frame draws the eye. Then, one might glance at what is in the foreground, but the mind processes it as merely fish or birds, and so one moves to the ship in the background. 'Ah,' one says to oneself, 'a storm is coming.' It is only upon further reflection—or upon seeing the title—that other details pop out, and the true meaning of the picture appears."

She shook her head. "It's distressing. And moving."

He smiled. "I'm glad to hear it. Let me take you to the café for a cup of coffee or tea, and give you a moment to sit and recover."

"Thank you."

Only after she was comfortably seated and had a cup of coffee in front of her had he introduced himself as Professor Reed Edgerton of Harvard. They had enjoyed a pleasant chat and had exchanged emails.

Angie wouldn't have exactly called him a close friend, but she always looked forward to exchanging emails and messages with him over books and paintings. She usually stocked her art section based on his recommendations, and they had met at the museum for several art shows ranging from Matisse and Botticelli to photographs from the Lodz Ghetto by Henryk Ross. She always felt that talking to him improved her ability to see the world, in one way or another.

She pulled the books he was looking for and sat down to write him an email.

Reed, I saw your order on Nantucket books come in! Does this mean that you're coming to the island to look for the lost Monet??? Please do! I'd love to see you. Should I hold the books here or send them to you in Boston?

She stepped out of the stock room to find Aunt Margery squinting at the computer in front of her, reconciling the drawer and the receipts with what she'd rung up. Janet had left long ago. She'd probably said a cheerful "goodnight," too which Angie had completely missed.

"Aunt Margery?"

"Yes?"

"Thank you."

She smiled. "I wasn't going to sleep anyway. Did you need something?"

"It looks like Professor Edgerton, that art professor from Harvard, is coming out for the treasure hunt. And I want to know if you're fine with putting him up in our guest room."

"Certainly," her great-aunt said. "But remember, he's a very private man. I suspect that he's found another place to stay. Don't be too disappointed if he says he'd rather not."

Angie laughed. "You make it sound like I'm eight years old and having my first sleepover with my friends."

"'Some day you will be old enough to start reading fairy tales again,'" quoted Aunt Margery. "C.S. Lewis."

"I'll ask, anyway."

She added the invitation as a P.S. to her email and hit send, then cheerfully worked on packing up the rest of the books.

Chapter 2
WHERE BEAUTY LIES

It had started in late August.

In July, the owner of half the island, Alexander Snuock, had been killed. He had left everything to his only child, Walter.

Both men were voracious readers. Which meant that Angie's bookstore, despite being on such a small island, was always well-supported by the community. But Walter was a much nicer man than his father had ever been, and Angie had half-fallen for him during the whole horrible situation. His impressive height, wavy brown hair, deep, dark eyes, and crooked smile didn't hurt, either. There was something about that smile, and the sly sense of humor behind it, that utterly charmed her.

It was awkward dealing with him as the owner of her property, but not so much of a problem that she couldn't get over it. She had insisted that Walter deal with her business just like he would with anyone else's.

After reviewing the will, Walter had been shocked by how much of the island he now owned. He had complained to Angie that it would be a full-time job managing everything. She had joked that he could always just give away his new fortune and responsibilities, because plenty of people would be eager to be in his shoes. He had given her a funny look, and she'd worried that she'd offended him. But then he had grinned and said, "I would, but it would be a blow to my pride if they turned out to be better at this than I am."

He tried to split his time between Manhattan and Nantucket as fairly as he could. Despite his heavy caseload, there had still been enough time for the two of them to spend hours together talking about nothing in particular. They discussed books, current events, Broadway shows, how to run a bookstore, how to try a criminal case, the kinds of people they had both known in college, how strange family could be, and so on. It was bonding moments like these that made for a lifelong friendship—or an enduring romance.

Then, while going through his father's papers, he had found a folder that contained a newspaper clipping about a famous French painting that had been lost on the island. From the rest of the papers in the folder, it was obvious that his father had been researching the painting for years. He had made some progress, but hadn't found the painting by the time he died.

The painting was an oil on canvas from 1864, about two and a half by three feet large, called *Boats at Sunset, Saint-Adresse*. The painter was Claude Monet, a French impressionist painter who was most famous for his paintings of water lilies. Monet had been known to take a small boat out onto the nearest body of water to paint boats and sunbathers. The painter's style was so quick and full of dabs of paint that he was able to capture his impression of a scene rapidly, rather than requiring his subjects to hold still for an entire afternoon, or even weeks' worth of sunny afternoons.

The lost painting was supposed to be of several sailboats with their sails down on a half-cloudy summer day, the kind where the fluffy sheep clouds of the early afternoon are starting to bump up against each other—not quite storm clouds, but getting there.

The other documents in the folder showed that the painting had definitely been brought to Nantucket.

The painting had originally belonged to the Nouges, a French family from Bordeaux who had been among Monet's earliest supporters. One of their sons attended the same school for the arts at Le Havre where Monet studied, and they became friends. Many years later, his grandson, Victor Nouges, arrived in Nantucket in 1918.

The Nantucket narrow-gauge railroad was inaugurated in 1881, but by 1917, it had closed. The equipment and rails had been sold to the French, who desperately needed the metal as World War I ended. Nouges was sent to inspect the purchase.

While he was on the island, he fell in love—with a woman who was already engaged.

The two had a passionate affair, but they both agreed that it had to come to an end. Victor Nouges returned to France with his purchase of a railroad, and the mysterious woman went back to her life and her fiancé. It was a love that was not meant to be.

However, in order to honor the memories of that love, Victor sent his amour a painting—the Monet. It was too valuable a painting, even then, for the woman to claim that it had been sent to her in mere admiration or friendship, so she hid it. She promised Nouges in a love letter that she had hidden it where it would never be found, but that she would be able to view it once a year on December 17th in order to remember their love.

The last letter in Alexander Snuock's original file was from Nouges, asking where his beloved had hidden the painting. The lady's response? Silence.

The painting was never found.

∽

On one August afternoon that was supposed to be nothing more than a harmless picnic in a park, Walter had handed her the folder.

"Here, look at this. I found it in my father's papers."

She had looked through the papers with widening eyes.

"Walter. This is amazing. Your father never mentioned it!"

She thought about all the books that his father had ordered, and tried to remember if he'd asked for anything on either Monet or the history of Nantucket. She realized that he had, right after she had first opened the bookstore. He had put in an order large enough that it didn't all fit in the wire basket on the bike she used to deliver books in warmer months, and she had to carry some of the books in a backpack.

"He did ask for several books that might have been research," she added. "Books on Monet and the history of Nantucket."

She had looked through her files, tracked down the books, and gone over them with a fine-toothed comb, but hadn't found a thing.

Then she had asked Aunt Margery, who was not only a notable gossip, but had investigated many of the darker legends of

Nantucket's history in order to include them in *The Little Grey Lady of the Sea: The Mysteries of Nantucket Island,* by the pseudonymous "David Dane."

Aunt Margery had grunted and started looking through her old notebooks. "I've heard that there was a lost Monet at some point," she admitted, "but I'd completely forgotten about it."

Angie had settled in to find the answer to a really good mystery—that fortunately was *not* a murder—and then, two weeks after the picnic, Walter had called her to explain the other half of his plan.

"I'm going to set this up as a public treasure hunt!"

"A what?"

She had taken a little while to be convinced, mostly because she kept imagining herself finding the painting and presenting it to Walter while everyone on the island applauded her. But really, Walter's idea was better for the island as a whole.

The rules went like this: Every official treasure hunter had to register with the Nantucket Chamber of Commerce. It was free, although they had to provide an admin at the Chamber with a valid email and cell phone number. Anyone who wasn't registered with the Chamber of Commerce couldn't win the prize—even if they found the painting. And locals couldn't win the prize either, which was disappointing, but understandable. An admin was available from eight a.m. to eleven p.m. every night at the Chamber of Commerce building. Walter had hired a couple of seasonal assistants to help, but all the regular employees had to rotate through shifts at the desk as well. The treasure hunters couldn't register online—they could only register from the island.

That last bit had been Angie's suggestion. She had taken one look at

Walter's proposed plan and said, "Someone online from, I don't know, China is going to win this."

"What?"

"This isn't going to be one of those things were the painting turns up in some random attic. It will be someone with a gigantic database who finds this, combing through random documents with a Google search."

His face had fallen. "But that won't help business on the island at all."

"Just tell 'em they can't win anything unless they're here in person. Like a door prize."

He'd laughed and changed the contest rules.

When the Chamber of Commerce employees found out they were stuck handling all the registrations in person, they'd almost thrown a fit—until Walter had offered them an extra assistant and reminded them that the painting, if found, would be hung in the building—at least at first. *Then* they'd fallen all over themselves supporting him.

One hundred thousand dollars in prize money over a one-point-five million-dollar painting. They had discussed the possibility that someone might find the painting and steal it, but in the end, Walter had decided that the potential benefits for the island outweighed the risk of losing the painting to a thief.

If the painting was never found, then the plan was to buy a reproduction and hang it in the Chamber of Commerce anyway, with a plaque explaining that it was an important part of Nantucket history (even if it was a fake).

∼

Then, after Walter had done an immense amount of work to prepare his plan for implementation at a big celebration just after Halloween, he had disappeared back to Manhattan and his legal work.

Angie, who had been soaking up the luxury of being spoiled by a thoughtful, kind, and charming multimillionaire, was suddenly left in a thoroughly single state.

It was unpleasant and annoying.

Theirs was no passionate love affair a là Victor Nouges and his unnamed lover, but it was a sane and wonderful thing—especially when compared to Angie's previous romance. Doug McConnell, an investment guru in Manhattan, had dragged her around to every fashionable restaurant as if he were proud to be seen with her on his arm. Meanwhile, he had taken all the credit for her work as an analyst, and to add insult to injury, had slept around behind her back. Yes, the more grounded nature of her relationship with Walter was one of its perks, in her opinion.

And just look at those lovers, anyway. Their passionate affair had led them exactly nowhere. Victor Nouges had gone home to France and his lover had probably married her fiancé. They had been left with fond memories of each other, and a painting.

Not a life together.

Angie's father was what was locally known as "Wandering Proutys," or the kind of Proutys who stayed put on the island to have kids before packing up and taking off for parts unknown. Her parents were currently still in Florida, which was "weird enough to keep them interested for a while." Angie was the other kind of Prouty, the "Staying Prouty," who left the island for a few years, then returned to settle down. Her family had been on and off the island for over a hundred and fifty years. Walter's family had been around for a similar length of time and were supposedly just as well known. Every local predicted that Walter would be one of the Snuocks that was known for his generosity and leadership. Not like his father, who had been one of the more selfish Snuocks, using wealth to control people instead of build them up.

But did that mean he would stay on the island or not? Nobody could say for sure.

Chapter 3
TIME ENOUGH AT LAST

Angie crashed that night when she finally arrived home. She lived in a shingle-sided tiny house near downtown with a bright teal door and about a million bookshelves stacked with mystery novels inside. Aunt Margery had already abandoned ship, and was sitting up in one of the comfortable chairs in the living room with a mug of cocoa by her side. It had started to sleet at some point, and the roads were slippery, but Angie had made the short drive home just for the sake of getting off her feet.

"How is it?"

"Everything's covered with ice," Angie said, unwinding the wool scarf from around her neck. "But it's not that cold. It'll melt."

"Tomorrow is going to be another busy day," Aunt Margery said.

Angie was too tired to care. "What are you reading?"

"*The Girl Next Door*, by Ruth Rendell," Aunt Margery said with relish. Aunt Margery tended toward darker crime novels. She was a huge fan of Truman Capote's *In Cold Blood*, and Gillian Flynn, Daphne du Maurier, and Patricia Highsmith were among her favorite authors. Angie was more of a puzzle-mystery reader. She liked tracking down clues, sorting out what kind of information was valid and what wasn't, and examining multiple possibilities.

It made sense. Angie had been a financial analyst for a high-powered Manhattan investment firm. Aunt Margery had been the town gossip.

And a writer of local ghost stories and legends, Angie reminded herself. *Don't forget that.*

"What about you?" Aunt Margery asked.

"I'm too tired to read," Angie yawned as she started for the stairs.

Aunt Margery's eyes widened, and she put her book down, one finger tucked into the spine. "Agatha Mary Clarissa Christie Prouty, one always has time to read." Aunt Margery exclaimed.

Angie snorted. Her great aunt was one of the only people who ever called her by her full name. And it usually happened in instances like these, when Angie's priorities got a bit tangled.

"I did hire an assistant," Angie retorted.

"Have you thought about two?"

The next morning, Angie arrived at the store at six a.m. as usual and assessed the damage. It wasn't as bad as she had thought when she'd locked up the previous night. The floors weren't covered with trash, the windows only had a few smudges on them, and she still had enough espresso to make it through a busy morning.

And Aunt Margery had done the books last night.

"Bless you," Angie whispered as she realized it.

A weight lifted off her shoulders, and suddenly everything seemed ten times better than it had a moment ago. She ran a vacuum brush over the wood floors, wiped a few of the worst prints off the front door, scratched Captain Parfait to his heart's content, and made herself a macchiato, swirling a snowflake pattern lazily into the foamed milk.

Janet wouldn't be in until one. Angie was on her own for the morning shift.

She double-checked the pastry case. It was empty, clean, wiped down. She checked the fridge again, then went into the stock room to see if Janet had left the leftover cupcakes anywhere. She couldn't see a single one.

She must have taken them with her. Why not? Hungry college-age girls would eat anything, even fruitcake.

Josephine arrived a few minutes later in a small brown Toyota. It was still too cold and icy to venture outside on bicycles, which was also Jo's favorite form of transportation. The trunk popped on the back of the car.

Jo had gone through several hair colors since July and was currently sporting red and green stripes in her mohawk. She said the kids liked coming into the bakery and seeing the different hair colors.

"You're not going to dress up like an elf, are you?" Angie had teased.

"I just might, smarty-pants."

Despite being an excellent baker and a sharp businesswoman (far more practical than her twin Mickey, that was for sure), Jo still had a wild side. Angie loved her for her directness and honesty.

"Sweets to the sweet," Jo announced as she came through the door. She had a single jingle bell tied to her Doc Martens, and her thumping boots sounded more like the Ghost of Christmas Past than a merry little elf as she walked.

"More cupcakes?"

"How did the other ones go last night?"

"I think they sold well. But it was so busy that I didn't notice, honestly."

Jo stuck her lower lip out. "You wound me."

"There weren't any leftovers this morning after Janet cleaned up. But I think she took whatever was left with her on a girls' night out. I'll ask her when she comes in this afternoon."

"I'm *so* glad you hired her," Jo said.

"What about the two of you?"

"It's busy," Jo admitted. "I should be asleep at three in the morning, but I have to get up to go to the bakery. At least when we run out of stuff to sell, we just close. So most of my work is done by ten a.m."

She yawned.

"Coffee," she ordered.

Angie laughed and made her a mocha with a few sprinkles of chili powder on top of the whipped cream. There was only one person in Nantucket who liked her coffee that way, but Jo was her best friend, so of course she stocked chili powder just for her.

"All right, I'm off," Jo announced. "Call if you need more product. Because the sooner it gets moved out the door, the sooner we can close for the day, and I'm wiped."

Angie finished her preparations, turned on a CD labeled "Flapper Jazz" on low, and unlocked the front door at six-thirty for her early risers. These tended to consist of retired gentlemen who wanted a newspaper and a cup of coffee while sitting in the café area by the window. Secretly, Angie thought of them as old tomcats like Captain Parfait, who generally avoided customers, but could be found at the front window most mornings until the tourists started coming in.

That morning, the assortment of customers was a little different than normal. First off, Jasper Parris, the director of communications for the Nantucket Chamber of Commerce, was waiting outside the front door as she unlocked it. He wanted to know if he could borrow an insulated coffee pot full of coffee—or more accurately, he wanted to borrow the coffee pot and buy the coffee.

She had a couple of extra coffee pots, so she loaned him one. Apparently the coffee machine at the Chamber of Commerce had died first thing that morning, and everyone in the building was in a state.

"If we run out before we get a replacement?" he said.

"How about I open a tab for you?" she asked. "Send one of the assistants over. That way you won't need to authorize them on a credit card."

He sighed in relief, his broad shoulders slumping. He was a fairly tall, well-built man with blond hair, round wire-rimmed glasses, and a mustache. He had an amazing collection of hand-painted silk ties. Today's tie was black and gold, with a black ear of wheat on the gold side and a gold ear on the black side.

"Where do you *get* all your ties?" she asked.

"I make them myself," he said, pulling the end of the tie out of his coat and flipping it back and forth. "I order white silk ties and hand paint them in my workshop. It takes forever, but it's a labor of love."

"I like them. Have you ever thought about selling them?"

He laughed deprecatingly. "What, and give up my romantic job at the Chamber of Commerce for the fame and fortune of running my own tie business?"

"Sure, why not?"

"Well, it's enough for me just to have a great conversation piece around my neck." He said with a grin, "Besides I have kids to support, so being a starving tie artist isn't really an option for me."

"I didn't know you had kids." she said.

"Yeah, two girls, 8 and 10, they live with their mom off island."

"Ah," she said sympathetically. Of course she wanted to know the whole story, but she'd do the decent thing and ask Aunt Margery later rather than bugging the poor man now. She poured Jasper an extra cup of coffee from one of the other pots so he'd have a full pot to take back with him to the office.

"Carol sends you her gratitude, by the way," Jasper said. Carol Brightwell was executive director of the Chamber of Commerce—the woman in charge. She had *not* been happy to hear about Walter's plan for the treasure hunt. Angie didn't think much of the woman. If it had been up to Carol, Nantucket wouldn't have had any events, period. She was always trying to reduce the effort she had to put in to various festivals and projects. Angie might complain from time to time, but Carol Brightwell seemed to be actively trying to sabotage the treasure hunt.

Why run the Chamber of Commerce if you positively hated tourists? One of the great mysteries on the island.

She wished Jasper luck. Her regulars had started coming in. Copies of the *Herald* and *Globe* sat on the counter along with a couple of *Wall Street Journal*s and *New York Times*. The local paper, *The Inquirer and Mirror*, was published on Thursdays, and it was only Wednesday, so she was out. *Yesterday's Island*, the free local paper, was supposed to be restocked daily at various businesses around town, but so many copies were being snapped up that Angie wasn't sure whether she'd get a delivery that day or not.

The regulars were stingy; they shared out a single copy of each paper and bickered over sports scores and discussed the obituaries like professional mourners.

Eight o'clock came and went, and the tourists started to arrive.

The first pair in were Mr. and Mrs. Beauchamp, a newly retired couple from Boston who struggled with what to do with themselves now that they weren't tied to their jobs. Mrs. Beauchamp, who had been a nurse for 42 years, was taking it worse than her husband, a former accountant. But Mr. Beauchamp was a thin, wiry man who had run several marathons, so he wasn't exactly someone who could sit still, either.

Angie waved at them. They had brought an RV over to the island after learning about the treasure hunt, and they planned to stay in it until the painting was found or they got bored—whichever came first. After their first visit, they had asked Angie whether they could park their RV in the back parking lot behind the bookstore while they were downtown. She had sent them to the property manager, who had given them the okay. So now they stopped by the bookstore for coffee regularly.

"Hello, Angie," Mrs. Beauchamp said.

"The usual?"

"If you would, please," she said stiffly.

Angie made her a cup of coffee with neither cream nor sugar, and one for her husband that contained both. She winked at him. He'd whispered to her that he wasn't allowed to have coffee, dairy, or cane sugar, but that his wife was allowing him to have one cup a day, "so make it a good one."

She warmed up two pastries for them and carried everything over to their little table. Mrs. Beauchamp gave her a genuine smile. "Thank you, my dear."

Mr. Beauchamp said, "I'm *sure* it isn't poisoned."

Mrs. Beauchamp mock-slapped him on the arm. "Charles!"

He chuckled under his breath. "You know, there was some suspicion that my wife poisoned someone, years ago."

"Oh, my," Angie said. She looked at Mrs. Beauchamp to try to gauge her reaction. The woman seemed to curl up on herself. Whatever this was, it was no mere setup for a bad joke. "Excuse me, I have to get back to things."

Mr. Beauchamp latched one hand onto her arm. "It was a rival...they were both working on the same research project at John Hopkins. He was a bad apple, though, through and through."

"Oh, Charles, now is *not* the time," Mrs. Beauchamp said primly. Her face had turned red.

"Used to harass all the girls." Mr. Beauchamp shook his head. "Wouldn't have blamed her if she *had* poisoned him, you know. But it turned out to be an accident—or mostly an accident— by this little side piece he was seeing behind his wife's back. Rat poison in the coffee, only she always made such bad coffee that he didn't notice it until it was too late."

"She had switched it with the sugar by accident," Mrs. Beauchamp said. "Although how you'd do that, I haven't the slightest."

"He put it in his own coffee," Mr. Beauchamp added. He let go of Angie's arm, patting it.

She knew she was gaping at him, but she couldn't seem to stop. She was completely flummoxed. "You're...you're just pulling my leg, right?"

He winked at her, and she quickly retreated in confusion. If discretion was the better part of valor, then she was going to just pretend she hadn't heard a word of that conversation.

The café sales had settled down. Since she had a moment, she decided to do a sweep through the store to see if anyone needed anything, and to make sure no one was trying to pry up her floorboards. If not, there were a thousand tasks that she could chip away at, like check her email and see if anyone had ordered any additional books. If she could stay caught up on her online orders, then she at least wouldn't have another night like the previous one.

She stopped at one of the mystery shelves, a hardcover catching her eye. It was one of Louise Penny's more recent novels. Looking around to make sure nobody was watching, she slid the novel off the shelf and held it in her hands, then carried it into the stock room and put it onto the small desk that held the inventory computer.

She was *going* to read that book. Aunt Margery was right. If she was going to own a bookstore and not read any books, was that any more of a life worth living than being an analyst for an investment firm?

She put a hand on her forehead, femme-fatale style. Okay, she was getting a little bit melodramatic. Of course she'd have more fun as a bookstore owner, even if she didn't get to read many books. And anyway, January was going to be dead. She could read then.

She heard a terrible groaning noise and ran back out to the floor to see what had happened.

A woman was pulling at one of her bookshelves, trying to literally yank it off the wall.

"Please stop that," Angie said. "If you're convinced that the painting is behind one of the bookshelves, all you need to do is take the documentation supporting your suspicion to the Chamber of Commerce, and they'll supervise the investigation."

The woman looked over at her with a blank face. "This bookshelf is a fake wall."

"I'm sorry, it isn't," Angie said.

"It is," the woman said, grabbing the side of the bookshelf again.

"It isn't." Angie led her to the end of the aisle, where they could both look from one side to the other. The bookshelf did brace up against a section of inner support wall, but by leaning from one side of the shelf to the other, it was easy to see that it didn't go anywhere.

The woman stared back and forth for what seemed a ridiculous amount of time, as if she were trying to find a way to prove herself right somehow—that a bookshelf leading directly from the Romance shelves to the Sci Fi section was somehow hiding a portal of some kind.

"And even if that were a secret passage," Angie said finally, "You would still need to get permission through the Chamber of Commerce first. Otherwise you'd risk invalidating the contest results."

"That's just wrong," the woman insisted.

"It's in the rules."

"But it's wrong."

Angie stepped away from her rather than lose her temper. Some people just didn't want to accept what was right in front of their eyes.

But the woman followed her. "You must work here."

"Yes," Angie said shortly.

"Tell me where the painting is. It's here. It has to be here."

Angie's curiosity got the better of her. "What makes you say that?"

What followed was a complicated explanation of the history of the building that Pastries & Page-Turners was in. Most of it even sounded correct. In short, this was *the very building* that Victor Nouges had used for his offices on Nantucket while he was assessing the condition of the railroad properties and helping negotiate the price of its sale.

"So...what makes you think that the painting is here?" she asked the woman.

"Because where else would it be?"

"The mysterious lover's home," Angie said.

"No. As an unmarried woman at the time, she would have been living with her parents. What happened was that Nouges left the painting in his former offices, where she would come to see it once a year."

"How would she have had access to this building?"

"If you look at the ownership records, you'll know that the building belonged to the Snuock family and stayed with them *to this current day*."

"You think the lover was related to the Snuocks?"

"Definitely. Don't you?"

Angie shook her head. "I only just took over the lease on this part of the building three and a half years ago. I know the Snuocks a little, and I know they've been on the island for over a century, but if the woman had been part of the Snuock family, wouldn't they have been suspicious when she came here once a year on the same day?"

"You're just not seeing the bigger picture," the woman said.

"I guess not." Angie held out her hand. She didn't necessarily want to introduce herself, but she wanted the woman's name so that if she did any damage, Angie could at least report it to the Chamber of Commerce. "My name is Angie Prouty."

"Of the Nantucket Proutys?"

"Yes. And you are?"

"Alayna Karner. I'm an archaeology student at NYU."

"I see. Modern archaeology?"

"No, ancient Aztec."

Angie nodded. The woman's inability to tell a supporting wall from a secret passage made a little more sense now.

"I wish you the best of luck," she said. "But please make sure you go through the Chamber of Commerce next time."

Alayna Karner sniffed and walked out of the bookstore. As soon as the door closed behind her, Angie's shoulders dropped and she sighed with relief.

The front door opened again, and within moments someone was saying in a plaintive voice, "Hello? Hello?"

A young woman with purple glasses was standing at the café counter with a terrified look on her face and an empty coffee pot dangling from one hand.

"How can I help you?" Angie asked.

"I'm from the Chamber of Commerce and Jasper sent me to pick up coffee, and there's a fight going on over there. I'm not sure if it's going to be okay or if someone should call 911, but either way we're out of coffee again and I don't know if maybe they'll all just settle down if they get something hot to drink."

Angie discovered the young intern's name, Marlee Ingersoll, and sent her off with two coffee pots full of coffee, one for each arm. Then she called Jasper's office number on the business card he'd left her.

"Director of Communications office, Nantucket Chamber of Commerce," a woman's raspy voice answered. "Where may I direct your call?"

"I'd like to speak to Jasper Parris, please."

"He's not available at the moment. He's in a meeting. May I take a message?"

The back door chimed and Angie twisted around to look. It was Jo, carrying a box of pastries.

"Tell him that Angie called from Pastries & Page-Turners. The extra coffee is on its way."

The voice gave a heartfelt sigh of relief.

~

By the time Angie had a moment to sit down and check her emails for orders, it was ten o'clock in the morning. Her early regulars had long since left the building and the tourists had flooded in. Most of them were curiosity seekers, far less serious about finding the painting than they were about finding a cup of coffee. Many of them asked for updates—had the painting been found? Were there any other clues?—but didn't seem to be too disappointed when there weren't any.

Then another one of the more serious treasure hunters came in.

Angie's radar for customer trouble went off the charts when the man walked into the shop. He was dressed in black leather and carrying a helmet under one arm. He wore mirror shades. He turned his head back and forth as he scanned the store, still holding the door open with one hand.

"Close the door," said one of the customers sitting at the café seats. "It's cold out there!"

He turned his head toward her, then released the door so that it closed, but not tightly. With one foot he kicked it shut.

He walked straight up to the café counter and set the helmet on it, almost knocking over the tea rack.

"Doppio," he said.

Angie pulled a double espresso, making sure that the crema was nice and thick. She served it up on a little tray with a small cup of carbonated water and a teensy adorable espresso spoon.

The man tossed a ten-dollar bill on the counter and walked off with the tray. Angie jotted the price of the espresso down on a napkin and folded it up with the bill—some people liked to open a "tab." If he hadn't spent it all by noon, she'd consider the rest a tip.

She kept her eye on him as she sat down at the desk she'd set up for Aunt Margery and stopped to check her emails for orders.

To her delight, she had received an email from Reed Edgerton.

Angie,

Delightful to hear from you! Yes, I will be on the island sometime later today (depending on traffic, of course), and I would be simply enchanted to see you. Regretfully, I have already arranged for a temporary residence and do not need to take advantage of your kind offer of a place to stay.

The treasure hunt for the lost Monet must be tremendously exciting for the island. However, it's not the treasure hunt directly that brings me to the island. I am on a different type of quest entirely. As you may not know, tracking imposters is a side hobby of mine—an unfortunate side effect of being true art appreciator. I recently have discovered some new information which leads me to believe that some rather magnificent impostors are finding their way onto Nantucket. They might even originate there! I look forward to boring you with my theories and documents over dinner. Would you be available tonight, perhaps? Hopefully the treasure hunters have left you a little time to eat with an old friend. As a reminder, I do not have any allergies or dietary constraints that you need to concern yourself with—in fact, I've decided to abandon my diet entirely for the next few days! And please do hold the books for me at the store; I shall pick them up forthwith.

Reed

She grinned. How she was going to find a way to ditch the store for several hours in order to eat dinner with Reed, she didn't know. But she'd work something out.

After replying that she would ask Aunt Margery and Janet to cover for her that evening (crossing her fingers even as she typed her reply), she heard someone clearing his voice on the other side of the desk. She looked up.

Mr. Motorcycle was trying to get her attention.

"Yes?"

"Do you have any books on the lost Monet?"

She went through her usual spiel, trying to size him up a little better as he spoke. He seemed deflated compared to his behavior as he had come in.

"So you're saying you have *no* books that might help."

"I'm afraid I don't."

His shoulders dropped. "Could I, uh, have another doppio?"

"Sure!"

She made him another as he brought his first tray over to the dirty dish tub that she left out for her more thoughtful customers.

She handed over the new tray and he hesitated. She waited. It looked like he was trying to work up the nerve to say something.

"Nothing's been found, has it?" he asked, sounding anxious.

"No, nothing," she confirmed. "If there are any updates, they'll be available at the Chamber of Commerce, although…" She waved at him to follow her back to the computer. Quickly, she looked up the Chamber of Commerce's website. "…There's nothing new on the site."

"How often do they update it?"

"Pretty often," she said. She suddenly remembered what the NYU archaeology student, Alayna Karner, had said about the building. *That* wasn't up on the site yet.

The man sighed again.

"Let me tell you something, though," Angie said. "I should call it in pretty soon, but you sound like you're having a bad day, so I'll share it with you first. It's not much," she warned.

"What is it?"

"It turns out Pastries & Page-Turners is in the same building that Victor Nouges once used as his office, back when he was inspecting the railroad materials and equipment that he planned to buy for the war effort in France."

The man's eyebrows rose.

"Is that a fact?"

"I'm pretty sure. I just learned it from another tourist, and it wouldn't surprise me. But I haven't had a chance to research it for confirmation."

"Why wouldn't that be on the website already? That sounds like elementary research right there, finding out where Nouges's office had been."

Angie felt her cheeks heat a little. "It's our first historical treasure hunt. There have been some bugs to work out."

He raised a hand. "Sorry, sorry. I didn't mean to...it's just frustrating. I've driven here all the way from Indiana."

"All the way from Indiana? Just for this?"

"I just got a divorce. I didn't have anything better to do."

"I'm sorry to hear it."

He shook his head. "I'm where a lot of men would want to be, if they could. Nothing and nobody to tie me down, a motorcycle to take me anywhere, and no rush to get there."

"I hope it's fun," Angie said.

"Not as much as I thought it would be. I should have done this when I was eighteen and wouldn't have gotten a crick in my neck from sleeping under the stars."

She didn't want to get tied down in the conversation, so she changed the subject. "Do you think you have a shot at finding the painting?"

"I'm a data analyst," he said. "I suppose I have as good a chance as any. I've been running analyses on births and deaths, trying to see if there are any anomalies around when the couple would have been together."

"You think there was an illegitimate child?"

"I think that if there was, then looking at births and deaths might be a good way to find out who the mother was."

"That's true," she said. She leaned back in her chair and thought about the queries she could run—but no. She wasn't eligible for the prize money, so she really shouldn't be doing the work. "It's an interesting approach, anyway."

"I thought so." Looking slightly less discouraged, he walked back to the comfy chair by the window that he had previously claimed.

Angie went back to the café area, checked that she wasn't running low on anything—the restock of pastries that Jo had brought earlier was a lifesaver—and did another pass through the store. Customers thronged the shelves, but in a good way: none of them were desperately trying to rip her shelves off their supports this time.

Mentally, she toted up the days since the contest had been announced.

The contest had officially started on December Fourth. And today was December Thirteenth.

With luck, things were finally starting to settle down a little.

~

At noon, Aunt Margery walked through the back door, took off her jacket, and rearranged the silk scarf across her shoulders. "Have you eaten?"

"I have not."

She handed Angie a paper bag that was both warm and fragrant. "I want you to hide in the stock room for half an hour and not come back until you have read at least three chapters of something."

Angie confessed that she had pulled a book off the shelves for just such a purpose, and opened the bag. Inside was a foam container of lobster bisque and a toasted cheese sandwich with bread at least an inch thick.

"Yum."

"You have an anonymous admirer," Aunt Margery said.

"It's Sheldon, isn't it?" Angie asked. Sheldon Table owned Sheldon's Shuckery along the harbor, and it was definitely his bisque.

"Close. Jeanette sends her regards."

Jeanette was Sheldon's French wife, who still managed to look elegant and dignified while married to the *worst* punster on the island. Or possibly the second worst—sometimes her jokes were so terrible they topped his. She was also an excellent cook.

"Does she want something?" Angie asked.

Aunt Margery made a face. "She would like to talk to you about some papers."

"About what?"

"She wouldn't tell *me*," Aunt Margery said, and walked toward the café area, where a pair of customers were waiting.

Angie retreated into the furthest corner of the stock room with the Louise Penny novel. One of the café comfy chairs had developed a wobble, and she'd moved it into the back so no one could hurt themselves in it. Carefully, she curled up in the chair, pulled out the bisque and put it on top of a pile of cardboard boxes, spread the paper napkin out on her lap, and began to read.

Bliss.

Chapter 4

AT WIT'S END

It seemed only a moment later that Angie heard her name being called, but she was already a hundred pages into the novel. She tore a slip from the paper bag and used it as a bookmark, then stood up and looked around. The stock room hardly seemed real, but that was pretty normal when she first came out of a book.

"Angie?"

"Coming."

She got up and walked toward the front of the store. Aunt Margery handed her the store phone. Angie started pacing back and forth behind the desk. "Hello?"

"It's Walter."

She put on a smile that felt a little stretched and thin. "Hello! Are you back?"

He paused before answering. "No, not yet. I just wanted to call and see how everything was going."

Mentally, she tried to make the adjustment from "work mode" to "talking to more-than-a-friend mode." It wasn't easy, partly because she had started to assume, before she met Walter, that she'd never again have cause to use the latter.

"Busy," she said, feeling awkward.

"Because of the treasure hunt?"

"It's going well. I mean, *really* well. And of course everyone wants to come to the bookstore and see what we have for research materials. Which honestly haven't been written yet."

"An opportunity for a good writer to pen the whole sordid tale," he joked.

"Yeah, I'm sure it'll sell like hotcakes—after Aunt Margery knows what to write for the ending."

Aunt Margery, who had walked over to the café counter to ring up a pair of customers and make them some drip coffee, snorted.

"Aunt Margery's writing a book?" He sounded genuinely delighted.

"She will if I can nag her into it."

"Would you? I think it would make great publicity for the island."

Angie rolled her eyes. What she wanted was a romantic conversation where Walter told her how much he missed her and wanted to see her again,. not a business conversation where they talked about marketing strategies for Nantucket Island. She had just gotten in the right frame of mind for talking to a more-than-friend, after all.

Not that she was willing to hang up or anything.

"It would," she agreed tactfully.

"Or you could write it."

"I'm...I'm more of the fiction writer type," she said, completely out of the blue. But it felt right.

"Murder mysteries?"

"Maybe. I haven't thought about it too much. And it's not like I have time right now."

"I think it's a great idea."

Her face heated. Both because the idea was a more than a little overwhelming, and because she was embarrassed about the uncharitable thoughts she'd been thinking just a few moments before.

"Thank you," she said, trying to keep her voice even.

He chuckled. "Well, I can only apologize for dropping such an unexpectedly large amount of extra work on everyone this holiday season. I wasn't thinking. I've been hearing from a few secret sources at the Chamber of Commerce that what I've done is completely unforgivable."

"I wouldn't say *that*," she said.

He laughed again. "Because you're too tactful to say something like that!"

"I don't have to be tactful if I don't want to," she said. "I can be *very* rude if I need to be."

He chuckled while she spoke. "Angie, you are one of the most delightful people I have ever known, do you know that?"

"I am *not* delightful," she said, but she was smiling.

"Positively delightful."

She rolled her eyes again. But of course she was flattered, and just a little tongue-tied.

"All right," she said after a moment, "You're forgiven."

"Whew. All right, I have to go now. But I'm glad to hear your voice."

"Me, too," she said. "I hope everything goes well with your cases."

"Thank you. Pick out a few books for me, would you?"

"What would you like?"

"Surprise me."

Now it was her turn to laugh. "People *hate* surprises. They just want someone to pick out the perfect thing that they would have wanted, if only they had known how much fun it would be beforehand. But I can do that."

"That...sounds wonderful."

He sounded genuinely touched. They said their goodbyes. Angie hung up, feeling refreshed.

"How's Walter?" Aunt Margery asked.

"Stressed," Angie said. Now that she wasn't overwhelmed by trying to keep up the witty banter, she realized that it was true. His voice had sounded strained. "He says he's sorry he dumped all this extra work on everyone without warning and that they're having a huge meltdown over at the Chamber of Commerce over it. He thinks you should write the story of the Lost Monet once we figure out the location of the painting and so on, and that I should write mysteries, and he also wants me to put together some books for him to read the next time he can come back."

"Mmm," said Aunt Margery. "I had been thinking about writing up a few posts for the Chamber of Commerce blog. What we know, what we don't know…'The mystery unravels' kind of thing. But I hadn't been thinking about a book. Tell him I think it's a fine idea." Her mouth curled up on one side. "A mystery writer? You?"

Angie said, "Why not?" She was feeling just a bit defensive about the idea now.

"Why not indeed?" Aunt Margery said. "Romantic suspense. The lovers are being pursued and it's a race against time between the killer and a nice juicy sex scene."

"Aunt Margery!"

"Or a cat mystery. Captain Parfait and the Case of the Missing Bookmark."

Angie rolled her eyes. "How about a nice puzzle mystery?"

"Yes, that sounds about right. Something that can be solved using the leetle gray cells, no?"

They both laughed.

"The mystery of the missing pastries," Angie said. "The detective with the butter stains on his shirt stands in the room full of caterers and says, 'The culprit must be…me!'"

"Or one of those funny ones where the narrator did it," Aunt Margery said.

"*Not* for my first mystery," Angie said. "Those are too hard."

"The butler did it."

"Dvoretskiy," Angie said.

"What?"

"That's the Russian word for butler. I'll just name the butler Dvoretskiy. Brilliant."

Aunt Margery tossed a wadded-up napkin at Angie as she chuckled and left to check on the customers. She'd have to thank her great-aunt later. Reading a book—and talking to Walter on the phone—seemed to have put her in a better mood than she'd been in for over a week.

~

Janet arrived on time and with a great attitude. Angie talked to both her and Aunt Margery about going out to supper with Reed Edgerton and asked whether they thought they could handle the store if another rush of customers came in.

They both *claimed* they would be fine without her, but Angie couldn't help worrying that they wouldn't be. Something might go wrong. She started giving Janet a list of instructions that were completely hypothetical, as in, "If someone comes in with Canadian money, don't accept the money, unless they look really desperate or they can't pay for it otherwise and then go ahead and take it anyway." She was listening to herself talk, and it even sounded ridiculous to *her*.

Finally Aunt Margery took Angie by the arm and said, "The Chamber of Commerce called."

Angie couldn't remember the phone ringing, but then again she might have missed it while trying to explain to poor Janet what to do if a customer wanted a book that wasn't available in the store and how to order it on the computer, in case Aunt Margery had to step out for a moment. As if Janet wasn't competent enough to write something down on a piece of paper.

"They called?" Angie asked stupidly.

"Yes. They called, and they desperately need more coffee, and they can't send anyone over right now."

Angie said, "I'll just step over there, pick up the empty pots, come back here, refill them, and—"

Aunt Margery turned Angie bodily toward the coffee pots. "Janet just made some coffee. Take two pots and go."

"But then you'll be short."

"We'll be fine."

Aunt Margery said it in such an annoyed tone that Angie finally picked up on the hint. They were giving her an excuse to leave. She had been at work since 6 a.m. in the morning, and had planned to work until it was time for supper with Reed. Then she had planned to come back and close up the store, staying until at least midnight again. *Then* she would do it all over again the next day.

She took a deep breath and said, "Did they want anything else?"

"No."

Angie put her jacket on, picked up the two coffee pots, and headed out the front door. They were both the vacuum-pump type of pots that would stay perfectly warm on the short walk to the Chamber building.

It was a cloudy, overcast day. She'd vaguely registered the weather at some point, but when that was, she couldn't exactly remember. There were a lot of things that she couldn't exactly remember. The last time she'd been so spacy had been at her old analyst job. There had been just too many things going on at the same time, all the time, and her brain hadn't been able to keep up.

She sighed and watched the steam billow up in front of her face.

She needed to relax, calm down, figure out what policies to put in place so that she wasn't constantly driving herself up the wall all the time like this. Hiring Janet had been a good step forward, but she hadn't sorted out what she wanted Janet to do, or how much responsibility she should delegate to her.

Angie rolled her shoulders and kept walking.

Janet was working at the bookstore while she was staying on the island with her father. She said she had no plans to find work on the mainland. What did she want to do with her life? When Angie had hired her, she had only been grateful that Janet would work for her—period. The fact that she was so reliable and level-headed was a bonus.

Why did Janet want to work at a bookstore? She liked to read, Angie knew that, but what? She'd asked during the interview but now she couldn't remember. Not mysteries. Did she want to be a writer? Did she want to be a librarian? Did she want to be a bookstore owner?

Finding out Janet's hopes and dreams would be essential to finding out what Angie could or could not ask of her. What if she liked numbers? She might be trusted with some of the bookkeeping. A writer? Then book ordering wouldn't be a bad idea.

She'd have to fit the girl's talents and interests to ongoing tasks that she could do in her down time. That way, Janet would have extra skills to take to the negotiating table at her next job and a better idea of what she liked and what she didn't. Angie, meanwhile, could hand over some of the tasks that were eating up her brainpower and spend more time helping customers—and figuring out bigger business questions.

This huge, seemingly unending rush caused by the constant flood of tourists onto the island for Christmas *and* the treasure hunt wouldn't last forever.

And then what? Did Angie want to try to grow the business? And if so, how quickly? Did she want to keep her stock relatively general, or should she start specializing? And what if she expanded the business to become a small publisher of local books, like a book on the Lost Monet? She could do that, she knew. She had a number of bookstore owner friends on the mainland, and she was on a number of mailing lists, newsletters, and message boards. A lot of other bookstore proprietors were discussing the possibility of opening small presses on the side. One or two had already started working on it.

And it was making her jealous.

She could either hang onto every little detail at the bookstore, or she could learn to give simple, clear instructions to her employees and start building a rapport of trust and support with them.

Standing in front of the red siding and white trim of the Chamber of Commerce on the cobblestone street, it almost sounded easy.

∼

Inside was chaos.

The front desk was abandoned, and there was shouting coming from the hallway leading to the back. Shreds of paper lay on the floor. There was an overturned styrofoam coffee cup behind the hotel-style desk, which was topped with two small vases whose carnations had turned completely brown and wilted.

As Angie bent over to pick up the cup, someone burst through the door to the back hallway and said, "And how can I help *you*?" in a perfectly nasty tone of voice. The shouting in the back of the building didn't seem to have died down at all.

The woman glaring at Angie was one of those solid, frosted-haired women who could probably take down any given teenager in a wrestling match out of pure stubbornness. She had her arms crossed over her chest and was wearing a teal green polo shirt and a silver watch with a wide band around her left wrist.

The pin on her right shoulder read *Tabitha Crispin*. Angie recognized the name, even though the two of them hadn't worked together before. Jasper usually handled everything having to do with the bookstore during festivals and other community events.

Angie decided to go with the simple answer. "Coffee," she said.

"We're out."

She pointed at the two coffee pots that she had left on the desk in order to pick up the fallen coffee cup. "Refills."

Tabitha's face softened. "Oh. You must be from the bookstore. Jasper said something about that."

"Yes. Angie Prouty."

"Margery's grandniece."

"Yes."

They shook hands. Tabitha's handshake was firm and warm, humid but not quite sweaty. Angie smiled. Tabitha's face stretched. Angie couldn't quite call it a smile, but at least the woman was trying.

"Is everything okay? Is there anything I can do?" Angie asked.

"We are at wit's end," Tabitha announced calmly, as if it were a perfectly normal thing to say. "But no, thank you. You've already done enough. I mean, you've already done what I would have asked you to do anyway. The coffee."

"Okay," Angie said carefully. "May I pick up the empties? And when do you think you'll want some more?"

Tabitha took a breath and said, "I'll go back and get them."

She turned back to the hallway door and opened it. The volume of the shouting increased. Now the shouting was coming from only one person, a woman who sounded as though she were about to break into tears. Tabitha closed the door behind her.

A few moments later, Jasper emerged, his brows pinched together in the middle. He was holding both of her other coffee pots by the handles.

"I've been instructed to walk you back to the bookstore," he growled.

So another person was getting chased outside to calm down and walk off some steam.

"Thank you," she said. "I'd appreciate the company."

She took a more scenic route back to the bookstore, saying that she needed to stop at the bakery on the way back. After the first block, Jasper let out an enormous breath of air that puffed up around him like a cloud briefly before disappearing.

"So you've heard that we're having a meltdown," he said.

"What happened?"

"The registration computer went down."

"Oh, no," she said. Just the thought of it was raising the hairs on the back of her neck. Of all the things she could imagine going wrong, a computer malfunction was second only to a credit card machine losing its connection. "At the same time that you were out of coffee. No wonder."

"Everyone is freaking out," Jasper said.

"Is there anything I can do to help? You could write down everyone's details and come over to the bookstore, then enter them in the database there? Our connection should still be up."

She only knew that because she had been trying to show Janet how to check on book stock from Angie's distributor and backup distributor.

"No, no, if it gets that bad I'll just take everything home and do it overnight. Or maybe I'll try my hand at fixing the computer," Jasper said.

Angie nodded. She wouldn't argue with him—he knew she would help him if she could. Besides, she could totally understand the urge to handle everything herself. She wondered if Jasper was caught in the same dilemma she was: balancing issues of trust, training, time, and paranoia like a bunch of spinning plates in a circus act.

If so, at least it wasn't just *her*.

They continued walking.

"Ah!" Angie suddenly remembered Reed's arrival. "I have a friend coming to the island today, and I want to know if he's checked in yet? If you don't mind. If you don't remember, it's fine, but—"

"What's his name?"

"Reed Edgerton."

Jasper screwed up his face, as if trying to recall a face to go with the name.

"He's about this tall," Angie pointed at Jasper's sleeve, "with broad shoulders, a big bald spot, a salt-and-pepper beard, and more of a New York accent than a Boston one."

Jasper laughed. "That's not a very flattering description."

"He's also very perceptive and *very* drily funny, but he tends to clam up around strangers."

"I haven't seen him, unfortunately. I think I would have noticed. And...a name like Reed I would have noticed on the paper ledger we've had to start using."

"Oh well."

"A friend of yours?"

"I'd like to think so. But mostly I'm just someone to take to art shows, I think. He's an art history professor at Harvard."

As they walked toward the bakery, Angie told Jasper the story of how she had met met Reed. She was just concluding her explanation when they reached their destination.

"This will just take a moment," Angie said. "But I'll understand if you want to hand over those empty coffee pots and head back to work."

"I think they were trying to get rid of me for a while," he admitted. "I'd better not."

"Me, too," she said. "Aunt Margery practically kicked me out the door. Let's see how the Jerritt twins are doing, shall we?"

∾

The twins were sold out of their regular pastries and were, once again, making up large batches of cupcakes to carry their customers over until the next morning. They had established an assembly line for filling and frosting and decorating huge trays of cupcakes that spanned from one side of the back of the bakery to the other.

"Wow," Angie said. "Are you really selling all those cupcakes?"

"Except for the ones we're giving away," Jo said, adding dabs of blue frosting to the top of a row of white-capped blueberry cupcakes. Her apron could have posed as an Impressionist painting called "leaning over the bench at the bakery all day." Her forearms were almost as badly smeared with frosting. There was a long streak running up her cheek and into her hair, too.

"She made me make the same cupcakes two days in a row," Mickey complained. He didn't look up either. Being so much taller, he didn't have to lean as much and was correspondingly cleaner.

"They'll still be just as delicious," Jasper said. "Believe me, we would be in even worse trouble if you hadn't sent over those boxes yesterday."

Jo turned to glance at him, then went back to her blue swirls. "Heya, Jasper."

Mickey put down the pastry knife he'd been using and wiped his hands on a towel. He walked over to Jasper and shook his hand. "Ignore her. She's short on sleep."

"We all are," Jasper replied.

"Some of us cling to sanity more easily than others," Mickey said.

"I heard that," Jo said.

"I haven't had much time today," Jasper said, "so I haven't been able to do much searching, but it seems as though your guess was correct."

"Really?" Mickey said excitedly.

"Remember, even if the painting is found in the attic, you won't be able to claim the prize money."

Mickey made a face. "So, hypothetically, if that were the case, who *would* get the money?"

"No one," Jasper said.

"Lame," Jo interjected.

Angie wished she could have slapped a hand over Jo's mouth.

Jasper rolled his eyes, but Jo didn't seem to notice.

"That's the way Mr. Snuock set it up," Jasper said stiffly.

"I know. But it's still lame. No offense, Angie."

"None taken." It was impossible for Angie to take offense at anything that came out of Jo's mouth anymore. They'd known each other too long.

"We were discussing using the funds for a locals-only party," Jasper admitted. "But that would have to go through Walter."

"Okay, marginally less lame," Jo said. She straightened up, put down her piping bag, and stretched out her back. "You want me to box up a couple of flat boxes for you to take back with you?"

"Y-yes," Jasper said. "I hope you don't mind if I leave you here, Ms. Angie, but I think everyone will be much calmer if we have cupcakes for them to eat while they fill out their forms."

"That's fine," Angie said. She claimed the two coffee pots while the twins quickly boxed up a pair of flat boxes with a variety of cupcakes. Jasper left with not quite a spring in his step, but he definitely looked happier.

"What's this about a painting in your attic?" Angie asked.

"You know that Pastries & Page-Turners was the location of the office that Victor Nouges worked from while he was on the island, right?" Mickey asked smugly, clearly expecting her to give a shocked "no."

"Of course," Angie answered, like she hadn't just learned it recently from a customer.

Jo snorted. "I told you she would know."

"You did," Mickey said sadly. "Anyway, my guess is that the mysterious lady was one of the Snuocks. Otherwise, she wouldn't have had a chance to meet the handsome merchant who became her lover."

"I was thinking the same thing, more or less," Angie said.

"I told you," Jo said.

"And," Mickey said, determined to push through, "*I* think the painting is hiding somewhere inside one of the Snuock properties."

"Was the bakery here back then?" Angie asked.

"Yes," Mickey said, at the same time that Jo said, "No."

"Well? Which is it?"

"There *was* a building here," Jo said, "but it was remodeled heavily in the 1990s. If the painting had been here at the time, it would have been found then."

"Not necessarily," Mickey said.

"Have you checked the attic?" Angie asked.

"No," Jo said.

"She told me not to."

"We've made almost enough money to pay off the last of the loans," Jo said. "The sooner this painting gets found, the sooner the moneybags leave again."

"Christmas will take care of it," Mickey said.

"Just because we'll have paid off our debts doesn't mean we'll be set for January. You can never count on spring showing up when you need it. I am *not* taking out another loan just to stretch us from January to Memorial Day."

"I promise I won't tell anyone if I find it," Mickey said.

"You will. You'll blab."

The two of them argued until Angie realized they'd been doing it all day—if not all week—and would still be arguing about it until the painting was found.

Then again, they argued about everything.

"I'm headed back to the bookstore," she said. "Keep me updated, okay? And watch out for tourists. I had one try to pry my bookshelf off the wall, looking for a secret passage."

"Was there one?" Mickey said.

"Not unless you count the back of the other bookshelves on the other side."

"Aw, man."

Chapter 5

THE END OF AN ERA

Back at the bookstore, things were in a reassuringly good state. No shouting, no spilled coffee, and no bookstore employees running around with their hair on fire. Angie patted herself on the back mentally for managing the store so well. The influx of treasure hunters had been a shock to the system, but she had adjusted quickly and things were running more smoothly now. She needed to figure out how to delegate more responsibility to others, but she was making progress.

"Empties," she announced.

The two women both watched her for a moment, then glanced at each other.

Then back at her.

"You seem calmer," Aunt Margery said.

"I'm sorry," Angie said. "I got spun up and stopped thinking about how other people were feeling and just focused on how worried I was about the bookstore. I need more time to think about it, but I'm going to be working on how to hand over both responsibilities and opportunities to Janet without being such a freak."

Janet laughed, then came around the café counter and gave her a hug. "Thank you. I needed to hear that."

"I didn't realize how much I was stressing both of you out."

Aunt Margery let out a breath. "How are things over at the Chamber of Commerce?"

Angie decided not to ask her if she'd lied about the phone call. "Worse than here. Their registration computer went down."

Aunt Margery winced.

"I told them they could come over and use ours—the one in the back, I mean," Angie said, "But Jasper said he planned to take the registration slips home and enter them himself. They kicked *him* out of the office, too, so he walked with me to the bakery and took some cupcakes back with him to the office. I think that'll help."

"'Rivers know this: there is no hurry. We shall get there some day.'"

"Winnie-the-Pooh," Janet said.

Angie smiled. She really needed to get to know her new employee better.

"So am I allowed back to the store?"

"Yes," Aunt Margery said firmly. "What time are you meeting Reed for dinner, by the way?"

"Oops. I need to check."

She rushed to the back of the store, stopping only to help three customers find things on the shelves and to answer their questions.

Reed had sent her an email only a moment or two ago saying that he would be available at six-thirty if she was still interested, but didn't offer any more clarification on what his actual 'quest' was. She sent a quick reply, telling him to meet her at Sheldon's Shuckery in time for a six-thirty reservation. She knew he'd be there at least half an hour early, in case *she* was early. Sometimes the man's fastidiousness made no sense to her.

He emailed back almost immediately, saying that he had found the address and would be there, but that he wasn't on the island yet. He didn't offer the name of the hotel or B&B where he would be staying, and she didn't ask—he might have thought it was rude. He would either tell her or he wouldn't. She had seen the way he had tensed up at art shows when other acquaintances of his had asked him seemingly innocuous questions. He would answer politely but without revealing anything, and she could sense his annoyance radiating off him. He seemed to think that people should be able to have an intelligent, well-informed conversation without having to discuss irrelevant personal details, like one's job, where one lived, whether one had a family, etc. Prickly? More than slightly. But still charming.

She shook her head, smiling. She was no better than the nosy people that annoyed him. In her heart of hearts, she had already mentally set him up with Aunt Margery. She looked forward to introducing them to each other. Sparks would fly, one way or another.

She called the Shuckery and set up the reservation, then walked back into the bookstore.

"Six-thirty at Sheldon's," she told Aunt Margery. "We should be back by—"

Aunt Margery raised a hand. "You will not rush back. You get here if and when you get here."

Angie laughed. "Yes, ma'am."

It was four o'clock. She'd leave a little early, run home, and change into something a little more dressy.

Sheldon's Shuckery was an oyster bar on the harbor that was known for its good food and its terrible taste—in puns. Not only was Sheldon a character in and of himself, but he'd decorated the bar in Nineteenth Century Gothic, more or less. Where every other oyster bar in town went for nets, rowboats, and fishing bobs—or, well, Northeastern Pretentious—Sheldon's went for dusty old antique bottles behind locked cupboards with signs like, DO NOT DRINK—POISON, weird medical equipment, felt top hats, and a board supposedly from the trap-door of the gallows at Salem.

She arrived at six fifteen, concerned that Reed would already be there. He would be too polite even to wait for her at the bar. But to her relief, she'd beaten him to the restaurant. Right ahead of her was Tabitha Crispin.

"I'm surprised to see you here," Angie said.

"Everyone has left but Jasper," she said. "He's insufferable right now. Carol was afraid that she was going to kill him, so she sent us all home at five."

"What if a big group of tourists comes in?"

The look that Tabitha gave her told her that any tourists would, in her opinion, deserve whatever they got.

Angie explained that she was waiting for a friend. Tabitha told her to have fun and waved at a small table. The woman who'd been waiting for her there waved back.

Angie had no problem waiting for Reed at the bar rather than claiming a table. She told Sheldon, who was playing bartender alongside the regular one, that he could give her whatever he wanted. He made her a kir royale, a simple mixture of Champagne and crème de cassis—the specialty of the evening. She saw several other people with the aperitif at their tables or at the bar.

He was in a good mood.

"So," he said, leaning in conspiratorially, "you're out on an important date? Does Walter know?"

She laughed and leaned toward him. "No, Walter doesn't know!"

Sheldon stuck his lower lip out. "It's not actually a date, is it? You don't have a secretive bone in your body, Agatha Prouty."

"I really don't," she agreed. "Or *do* I?"

He chuckled. "My wife wants to talk to you."

"Yes, I got the message."

"Who *are* you meeting tonight? The suspense is killing me."

Angie told him about Reed Edgerton.

"So you think he has information on the painting?" Sheldon said.

"I'm not exactly sure. His expertise is in art, but he said he's not planning on hunting for treasure. I was hoping to get some clarity here at dinner. A registered tourist has to be the one to find it, so I can't imagine he's here just for the views and shopping," she said.

"Well, if he does give us some information on the painting, maybe Jeanette and I can *hire* a tourist and split the money with them, right?"

"Sheldon!"

He cackled, patted her on the shoulder, and said, "I'll keep an eye out for this fellow. He sounds interesting."

"He is," she promised him. "I think you'd get along like a house on fire."

"I hope not!" Sheldon pushed through the swinging half-door between the bar and the kitchen. Angie heard him calling for his wife, using the most ridiculous pet names. "Jeanette? Whoopie-Pie? My savory little sweet potato? My little crème fraîche?"

Angie sipped at her drink, checked the time on her phone, and half-turned so she could keep an eye on the front door.

No Reed.

It was six-thirty.

She told herself not to worry. She checked her messages and email, but there was nothing, so she finished the kir royale as she waited. Sheldon appeared, took the empty, and checked the clock over the bar, which was ten minutes fast.

"Everything all right?"

She gave him a smile that felt stretched and fake. If it had been literally *anyone* else, she wouldn't have been worried. Life had a way of affecting plans. But Reed hadn't called or sent a message. That wasn't like him.

Sheldon tilted his head. "Something *is* wrong," he said.

"He's normally early," she managed to say. Her throat felt tight. "I'm just being stupid."

"Listen to your instincts, ma chère," said a voice from behind her.

Jeanette was wearing an adorable apron covered with cute kittens chasing balls of yarn.

"Just call him," Sheldon said in agreement. "He'll understand that you're worried about him."

"I don't want to annoy him..." She sighed and pulled out her phone. Once again, no messages. She dialed his number; it rang several times and went to voice mail. She left a message.

"Where is he staying?" Jeanette asked. "We can check with them to see what time he came in."

"I don't know," Angie said. "He's so private...I got a message from him about four o'clock agreeing to meet me here at six-thirty, but saying that he hadn't made it onto the island yet."

Sheldon and Jeanette looked at each other.

"He would have to be on the four-ten Hy-Line or the five o'clock Steamship," Jeanette said. "Otherwise, how could a punctilious man be sure of arriving on time in order not to disappoint a young lady? He would have said something otherwise, I am sure." She turned to Angie. "Did he bring a car? Or did he plan to take the shuttle? Or rent a car?"

"I don't know," Angie said. "He didn't say."

"I'll call Lexie at the Hy-Line desk," Sheldon said. "She should be able to tell me about the Steamship ferry, too. Angie gave me a good description. He sounds like a real character."

"You are a real character," Jeanette said. The tall woman leaned over and kissed her husband on the top of his balding head. "And thank you for coming to the rescue."

Sheldon walked back into the kitchen with a smile on his face.

"He's going to walk through the door any second now," Angie said. "And all this worry will have been for nothing."

"That is true," Jeanette said. "But then again, it is better not to let worry fester too long. While you are waiting, won't you come with me to the office? I wanted to show you something. It would make a good distraction, and someone will tell us if your friend arrives while we cannot see him."

Angie took a breath. "Of course. What's it about?"

"Why, the treasure hunt," Jeanette said. "What else?"

As they threaded their way through the close-packed but seemingly random tables scattered through the restaurant, surrounded by the comfortable chatter of people eating good food in good company and the muted sounds of an accordion and a woman singing in French, Jeanette said, "I have been going through the boxes of old documents that have been in the house since forever. You know that Sheldon, he hates to throw anything away. Ever. But he cannot organize anything. He pushes it all into the same boxes until they get full, then carries them up to the attic without any kind of label whatsoever. I have found love-letters from a girl that he loved decades ago next to telephone bills and receipts for shoes. So romantic! They were not even tied up in a ribbon."

She shook her head. Angie could imagine Jeanette sorting out long-lost love letters, tying them up, then teasing her husband about it later. "You are never allowed to have an affair, because you would need your wife to organize it well enough to keep it secret from your wife!" Something like that.

"But what is important is that he also threw all the other paperwork he found into boxes, and those are in the attic too," Jeanette was saying. "So that one moment, I am reading a receipt from 1985, and the next, a page from a ledger a hundred years older than that."

"Is the Shuckery that old?" Angie asked.

"Oh, yes, it is older in parts and not so old in parts. The part that extends over the water, it is not that old; it must be replaced from time to time. But the main part of the house that is now the rear of the restaurant, that is very old. It is like walking through the small rooms of a house, no? Which makes it very comfortable to have privacy."

Angie nodded. The whole building felt old, or at least not new, but the back part of the building had a narrow hallway and doors so low that some people had to duck to go through them. The doorways were capped with beautiful leaded glass transoms.

"We are sure *that* part goes back to at least 1849, because we have a bill of sale from that year. But it is most likely older than that, because it was a bill of sale, yes? Not records of construction."

The office was in one of the rear-most rooms and was stuffed at Angie's head-height with what looked like an endless row of ledgers. In other words, historical documents.

Jeanette had to duck a little to reach the back of the desk. She unlocked one of the drawers and pulled out a file folder.

"I had it ready for you to look at," she said.

"Jeanette, why do you want me to see it? You know that I can't win the treasure, either."

Jeanette winked at her. "I said to Sheldon, 'Angie, she would know what to think about this.' I suggested it. And he said yes."

Angie sat in the small chair in front of the desk. Jeanette sat before the computer and started tapping away at the keys.

Angie flipped open the file. The first piece of paper was a fragile newspaper clipping about the founding of the Nantucket railroad in 1881. Angie hardly dared to touch it. The railroad had been a narrow-gauge railroad, which meant that, for the most part, it had never been meant to ship commercial goods or anything heavy, like rock or coal. The train cars would be too small and unstable for that. No, it was a tourist line.

The train engine's name was "Dionis," she read, in honor of the wife of one of the original settlers on Nantucket, Tristram Coffin. Having grown up on Nantucket, Angie could vaguely remember the name. She wanted to say it was around the 1650s or so when he and his wife had arrived on the island. That's right! He was one of the original group who had bought Nantucket for something like a hundred dollars and a beaver hat. Only that was before dollars, so it was probably some comparable sum of British pounds.

The train was built to entice tourists to travel to, and around, the entire island. Carefully, she flipped to the next sheet of paper, then held her hands out of the way. She felt almost sacrilegious touching paper this old. The most valuable paper she normally dealt with was signed first editions from the twentieth century!

The next piece of paper was another newspaper clipping, this time announcing an attack on the railroad by locals only months after the train had opened to the public. Reading between the lines, Angie guessed that local cabbies had been to blame. No one had been arrested, at least at the point the article was written. She'd have to do more research if she wanted to find out whether the mystery had ever been officially solved. If she had to guess, she'd say that it hadn't been, but she suspected that the culprits had received a private talking-to and may have had their feet held to the fire to donate money to the island.

Another clipping bragged about the one-year anniversary of the train, and how it had carried over 30,000 passengers.

"Wow, Jeanette. This is some amazing stuff that Sheldon has been saving."

"Keep reading."

Another clipping had sadder news. In 1895, the railroad closed down after a series of expensive repairs necessitated by repeated flood damage. The Nantucket Railroad reopened soon afterward under a new company name, the Nantucket Central Railroad Company.

Aha, Angie thought. She knew enough about financial analysis to smell a business reorg in favor of private investors when she saw it.

"Jeanette," she said.

"Eh?"

"Do you know who the investors in the Nantucket Central Railroad Company were?"

"No, there was nothing in the papers about that. At least, nothing that I have found yet."

"Did Sheldon's family own this building all the way back then?"

"I do not think so. What are you thinking?"

"That I might look up who owned the building at the time, and who the investors in the Nantucket Central Railroad Company were."

Jeanette gave a little shrug. She wasn't obsessed by mysteries, but rather by a sense of order. And *that* was why Angie was now involved. She would bet twenty bucks that Jeanette had found the papers and taken them to Sheldon, Sheldon had hinted that Jeanette should talk to Angie, and Jeanette had decided that it was her own idea to do so. Sheldon could be subtle when he felt like it. Not that many people would have guessed, given that he usually wasn't.

Angie wondered if the locals were beginning to consider her their local sleuth. She had played a pivotal role in unraveling the mystery of Alexander Snouck's death, and she did love to solve problems. Angie dismissed the idea and focused back on the next piece of paper Jeanette was showing her.

The railroad changed over from coal to gasoline engines. The first engine was tested in 1907, and a second engine in 1910. Which made sense, sort of. Internal combustion engines were in development during the eighteenth and nineteenth centuries, and the Ford Model T would have appeared on the market sometime around…1910, maybe? She'd have to look it all up. She was solid on things like the publication date of *The Phantom of the Opera* and Joseph Conrad's *The Secret Sharer*, but the history of automobiles, not as much.

But the changeover to the gasoline engine went along with the decline of the railroad, and no wonder. As the number of automobiles on the island—including trucks and buses—grew, fewer and fewer people chose to ride the rails, which were limited by the railroad tracks in a way that busses or private cars weren't.

In 1917, the railroad closed for good. The end of an era.

The next clipping was about Victor Nouges and his father, Albert. Albert Nouges, and the Nouges family in general, owned a large shipping company in France which was working with the Allied forces. The clipping bragged about the family's connection to the famous painter Claude Monet through Victor Nouges, who had also trained as an artist.

"We hope that Mr. Nouges will help bring French culture to the island of Nantucket," the article concluded.

There was no mention of any paintings accompanying him, by Monet or anyone else.

Angie turned to the next piece of paper. It was in much better condition than the previous ones, a full sheet of actual paper rather than the ragged newspaper pulp of the clippings. The paper was thick and smooth with linen fiber in the paper, and had been folded over on itself in fourths.

Angie unfolded it carefully.

It was a large ship's manifest, dated 1917, listing passengers on the ship SS *Puy de Sancy* as well as the cargo.

Jeanette stopped typing and said, "Do you see it?"

Angie skimmed over the page. "No...wait." She put her finger on one of the lines with a big swooping "M" on it. *Monet.* "The line showing that the painting was shipped here?"

"Oui."

Angie skimmed through the rest of the manifest but didn't notice anything else that stuck out. "I can't make out all the writing on here," she said.

"Moi non plus."

"Do you mind if I take a picture of it and try to keep working on it?"

"Why? There is nothing else to be found on that paper."

"It's too tempting," Angie said. "All that history, right in front of my face, and I can't read it."

Jeanette laughed. "Then take a picture! I would not be the one to stop you from your obsessions."

Angie took out her phone and photographed the manifest several times.

The next page was an insurance document for the painting. It stated that the Monet was valued at five thousand francs and owned by Victor Nouges.

Even though the document had been typed, Angie took a pic of that one, too.

"You know," Angie said, "The Jeritt twins, mostly Mickey, that is, seem to think that the painting might be in the attic of the bakery."

"Yes, the bakery is very old," Jeanette said. "Did they look?"

"No, Jo wants to make sure the tourists stick around long enough to pay their bills first."

Jeanette laughed heartily. "Sometimes, I think she would have fit into my French family very well. We have always been known for our heartless bread-bakers."

"Heartless?" Angie asked.

"Oh, the worst," Jeanette agreed. "During the Revolution, my family was held up to the wall with bayonets while the people took all the bread. The family story is that my ancestor threatened to start baking moldy flour into the bread on purpose if they made him bake for the Republic without pay." She drew a line across her throat. "Shhhick!"

"No!" Angie said.

"Mais oui. But when Napoleon came to power, we came back into respect, because everyone likes good bread. But I, I am the black sheep of the family, and I am only a cook. The twins, their bread isn't as good as my family's bread, but what can you do? The flour here is terrible. I am sure that if they had the same flour we have in France, they would soon make bread *almost* as good as my family's."

Angie wasn't sure if Jeanette was pulling her leg, but it was probably better to pretend that she believed every word.

"That's amazing," she said.

"And so you must tell me what you have learned."

"Nothing, yet," Angie said. "We knew the painting had come over here, because of the clippings that Walter found. The painting arrived and was displayed to the public in 1917, for reasons that had nothing to do with the mysterious lover. It sounds like the people of Nantucket hadn't been expecting the painting at all. It just came out of the blue. Why Victor Nouges brought it with him in the first place was a mystery. And then, just before he left, the painting disappeared. That's all we really know for certain."

"And?"

"And..." Angie closed her eyes and imagined the painting sitting on an easel, being shown off to everyone in the town. "And why did Alexander Snuock, or someone in the Snuock family at any rate, save all those clippings that Walter found? I think everyone on the island has the same feeling—that the Snuocks had to be involved."

"The family was powerful then, too," Jeanette said. "So they had to be involved somehow, yes?"

"But how?"

"That is what we want to know from you."

Angie said, "I don't have enough information yet."

"But this helped?"

"I don't know."

"But you are supposed to be the great detective!" Jeanette exclaimed, laughing. She leaned forward and kissed Angie on the forehead. "Don't let it trouble you. You will keep looking around and asking questions, and everyone will tell you their secrets. The painting, it will be found eventually, and if it is not found until after the Jerritt twins have made enough money to keep the bakery open, est bien, that is how it will be."

"I'm not hiding anything," Angie said.

"I did not say you were, ma chère."

Angie checked her phone. Still no message from Reed.

∼

Sheldon said, "It's seven fifteen, and you look like you're starving. Any word?"

She shook her head. She had called Aunt Margery while she was still in the office. Her great-aunt had said that everything was fine at the bookstore, but that she hadn't heard anything from Reed either. Angie checked her email. Nothing.

"No, and I'm really getting worried."

Forty-five minutes late, and Angie was starting to think that maybe Reed had not made his ferry.

"The ferry didn't crash or anything, did it?" she asked.

"Heh. No," Sheldon said. "I called the office like I said I would, but they said they hadn't seen anyone that looked like him. Although Lexie did say that it had been really busy and someone might have missed him, especially if he came over on the Hy-Line. It's always easier to remember someone with a car or a bike."

Angie nodded.

He patted it and said, "Why don't you sit down and have something to eat?"

"I should really wait for him. Forty-five minutes is late, but perhaps something came up."

"A cup of coffee then?"

That, she couldn't turn down. And then at eight-thirty, she couldn't turn down a bowl of chowder and a small loaf of heated French bread with butter.

At nine o'clock, she paid her bill, gave Sheldon and Jeanette a hug, and drove back to the bookstore. A car she didn't recognize sat in the back lot, and for a moment, her spirits soared. She ran to the back door and burst inside, looking around eagerly.

But Reed wasn't anywhere to be seen.

Her hopes deflated.

Aunt Margery said, "Nothing?"

"No, nothing."

It was nine-fifteen and the bookstore was still busy enough to keep it open, but nowhere as bad as it had been the night before. The pastry case was almost empty, with only a few of the blueberry and bourbon cupcakes left.

"They must not have made fruitcake tonight," Angie said to Janet.

"No, they did," Janet said. "After the way they sold out last night, good thing, too. At first everyone was like, 'Oh, *fruitcake*, yuck,' but then I cut one up into samples and passed it out and whoosh, gone like that. So I called them and said they should bring twice as many tonight. Those are gone already too, even though there weren't as many customers tonight."

Angie shook her head. "That's amazing."

"Fruitcake is really good," Janet said. "You should give it a try."

"I did, like twenty years ago," Angie said.

Janet laughed. "Well, I *think* they would have gotten better at fruitcake by now."

Angie glanced at Aunt Margery, who was struggling to keep a straight face too.

"I think it's the difference between store-bought and homemade," Angie said finally. "We always ended up with the kind that was as heavy as a brick, that people had been passed around for years, and that was so sweet with corn syrup that it was just yucky to eat after bite or two."

"Oh, yeah," Janet said. "That makes sense. Well then, this is totally one of those things that's better homemade."

Angie started going through the inventory and putting together an order, moving on autopilot. She stopped to pick up a piece of paper from the floor. It had a list of books on it with most of the titles scratched out, and one of them circled so hard that the paper had wrinkled around the pen marks. The books were all local titles. The circled one was about the Brant Point Light. *Light in the Dark* was written on the paper—a book that Angie suspected was *A Light in the Dark: Putting a Value on the Brant Point Lighthouse, 1746-1901*, by James A. Higley, Jr.

She remembered the book. The lighthouse had burned down multiple times early on because it had been constructed out of wood and the warning lantern had run on oil and kerosene. At one point, the lantern was a pair of poles and an ordinary lantern hanging between them, which must have been just about useless.

The list belonged to a treasure hunter, more than likely.

So why the lighthouse? It had definitely been in use in 1917 and 1918, so conceivably the painting could have been hidden inside it somewhere, but the book itself only went to 1901.

She checked the shelf. No more copies. When she got a moment, she'd look in the back and see if she had any extra copies. She should probably order some more, regardless.

∼

They closed at ten. Still no word from Reed.

Angie tracked down two copies of *A Light in the Dark* and set one aside for herself, then put the other one on the shelf. By ten-thirty, Janet had finished all her duties.

"Reporting in for any additional tasks, ma'am, yes ma'am," she said, appearing at the door to the stock room.

Angie opened her mouth to tell her that she was fine to go home—she really didn't want to pay overtime—but stopped herself. Hadn't she just promised herself earlier that she would spend more time getting to know Janet and finding out how she could help with the store?

"Janet, have a seat."

Janet made a pained face, and Angie laughed.

"Sorry, sorry! I forgot how that kind of thing sounds. I'm *not* firing you."

Janet exhaled, clearly relieved.

"I'm just mad at myself for not planning well. I should have figured out some training to do with you if we had the time tonight. And it's occurred to me that I'm not really sure what kind of...plans you have for yourself later. I mean, I know that's one of the questions that you get asked during a job interview, but I was so wired that I don't remember if I did or not, or what your answers were if I did."

"You didn't," Janet said. "I thought it was weird, but not too weird. You always seem so worried about being rude that I just figured you didn't want to pry."

"I'm nosy," Angie said. "My natural instinct is to pry, pry, pry. So I guess I was trying to hold back so I didn't freak you out."

She smiles wryly, and Janet laughed.

Then Janet drew herself up. "To be honest, I'm not sure what I want for the future. Do I want to stay on the island? Do I want to go somewhere else? I've never really had a strong, um, calling for anything. I didn't grow up saying, 'Oh, I dream of being a ballerina.' I like playing volleyball and softball, and I like reading books, and I like playing music, and I like animals, and—"

"Music?" Angie asked.

"Yeah, I play a little guitar. Really terribly. I don't practice enough. But I still like to do it. You know, just sit out on the back porch of my parents' house on the porch swing and play old songs. I played 'I'm So Lonesome I Could Cry' for a month straight, and my parents had to talk to me to make sure I wasn't depressed or anything. I just liked the way the beagle across the street howled as I sang."

Angie laughed.

"I don't write, I don't like to do crafts, I just hang around with my friends and complain about not getting enough dates," Janet said. "I've done all kinds of jobs. I've worked at a nursing home and a grocery store and a couple of restaurants and a clothing store. The only one I didn't like was the clothing store, but none of them really called to me. As soon as I had to go back to school, I'd quit whatever job I had and go back to Boston."

"What did you go to school for?" Angie asked. "Forgive me for having to ask *again*."

"No problem. I went to Brown in Rhode Island for Communications. My mom jokes that I was born to be in HR at some big company, but I think that idea stinks. I have friends at Brown that did that, and they have to deal with jerks all day, every day. You know who has to deal with it when someone's been watching stuff they shouldn't be watching at work? HR. Like, not even naughty stuff. I have one friend that had to fire someone for pirating movies at work. They could have gotten the company sued, but did they care? No. Out the door. The person had three kids, too, and was going through a divorce. Worst timing ever."

"I can see why you wouldn't want to do that," Angie said. She looked up toward the ceiling. "Okay, for the sake of the argument, what do you know about writing ad copy?"

"Ad copy? Sure, I've done a ton of advertising campaigns. I can't do the art, but I can usually pick some out that's okay."

"And what about…a social media campaign? Like running a twitter channel?"

Janet made a noise in the back of her throat and studied the tiles on the ceiling. "Well, first I'd have to write up a media plan and have you approve it. Because the worst thing is when you're stuck in a situation where you're trying to come up with advertising for someone and they just don't get it. They're like, 'Just make something and I'll tell you whether I like it.' And that's a fast way to spend a lot of money fixing mistakes and making changes. Nobody comes out of that happy."

"Would you like to work on something like that and see if it's something you want to do?"

"Sure," Janet said. "Why not? Only I don't really have a passion for it or anything."

"Sometimes passion isn't as relevant as we think," Angie said. "*I* thought I had a passion for data analysis, and here I am at a bookstore."

"So you must have some pretty good data about sales and stuff," Janet said, perking up. "If I could have it, that would make writing a media plan a lot easier."

"Let's try it," Angie said. "Step one, write up a list of what you need from me in order to come up with a media plan for Pastries & Page-Turners. Hypothetically, we could start on the plan in January, or in February after the store opens up again."

"You're closing the store?" Janet sounded panicked.

"Aunt Margery and I are going on vacation in the Mediterranean," Angie reminded her. Then she said, "Or…you could try running it yourself while I'm gone. Three weekends for Friday, Saturday, and Sunday is all, but they'd be long days so you could get some hours."

"Yes, please," Janet said. "I'm saving up to move out of the house. I'm twenty-three. I need to start moving forward with my life if I'm ever going to."

"Housing is expensive here."

"I know it. But if a few of my friends share a rental with me, we might be able to make it work."

~

Midnight.

Still no word.

Angie sat down to pet Captain Parfait, who head-butted her chin and curled into her lap. After a few moments, she forgot to keep petting him and stared out the window instead. The weather had turned wet again, and the cobblestones shone under the streetlights. It would be a cold drive home.

She hoped Reed was all right.

Chapter 6
PAST WIT'S END

She woke up in the dark, knowing that it was nowhere near time to get up yet. She'd been having one of those half-nightmares—not really scary, but saturated with anxiety and a sense of claustrophobia. She'd dreamed she was sorting through endless pieces of paper. In the dream, she knew that she had to find out something very important in the documents Jeanette had found. There was something that both of them had missed, and only the most scrupulous attention to detail was going to unearth what she needed to know. She remembered wishing she was a TV detective with a team of operatives who could do things like hack into computers to find the information she needed before the episode concluded, but nobody was around to help her.

Her stomach was knotted with worry as she opened her eyes and answered her cell phone before she even realized it was ringing.

"Reed, is that you?"

"I'm sorry, ma'am. This is Detective Baily from the Nantucket Police Department."

"Hello, Detective Bailey. I'm sorry, I just woke up."

"I know, ma'am," he said in a pitying voice, and she suddenly remembered that he was only five years older than she was. At least, Aunt Margery had said so once.

"Well Angie, I ran into Sheldon late last night, and he mentioned you were there in the evening. You were waiting for a fellow named Reed. Is that right?"

"Did something happen to Reed?" she said. "Reed Edgerton is his full name. He's from the Boston area."

The detective took a deep breath before delivering the news.

"I'm afraid something did happen to him. His body has been found in the harbor just off Children's Beach. We almost missed it. The tide was going out, and it was about to be carried out to sea."

Angie struggled to hold onto her phone. She felt like the dream hadn't ended. The tightness in her stomach transformed into a hollow ache and she fought back tears. "So he's... he's dead?"

"Yes, ma'am. I'm sorry Angie, Sheldon told me he was a friend of yours."

"Yes, I suppose we were friends. I didn't see him often, but.. this is so terrible!"

"Angie, I need you to come down to the station. We need to make sure that it's Mr. Edgerton for sure, although we did find his wallet on him. And we'd like to ask you a few questions as a formality."

"I understand," she said in a quiet voice. "I'll come right in."

She decided to take the road past Children's Beach on her way to the station. It was out of her way, but she wanted to see whatever she could.

The Chamber of Commerce building was still lit as she drove by. She could see the top of Jasper's head behind the front desk through the window. His round, wire-rimmed glasses flashed as he looked back and forth from the computer screen to something on the desk.

It was just past two a.m. Poor guy.

Four police cars were parked beside the beach, and she was directed around the area by a young policeman with a flashlight. An ambulance was driving away, its lights off.

She pulled over on the side of the road to collect herself. Reed had been such a wonderful man, and she was feeling more emotional over his death than she had expected. She wiped a few tears away and took a deep breath.

The police officer knocked on her window.

"Are you all right, ma'am?"

"Detective Bailey just called to tell me the news about Reed," she said. "I shouldn't have driven by here. I should have gone straight to the station, but I was curious."

He finally talked her into getting into his car and drove her the rest of the way himself before escorting her to Detective Bailey's desk. That meant she didn't have to talk to anyone at the front desk, and she was grateful for it.

Detective Bailey took one look at her and sent the officer off to bring her some coffee. Blowing her nose, she explained to him what had happened—that driving past the place where the body had been found had upset her more than she had foreseen.

"He wasn't...he wasn't a close friend of mine," she said. "But he was a friend. I was so happy that he was coming to the island."

"He was here for the treasure hunt?"

"Well... not exactly. He said he was coming for a some other 'quest.' He mentioned imposters. Reed was a Harvard Professor, and about as eccentric as you would expect him to be. There was something he was going to explain to me over dinner, and something he wanted to show me."

"What was he going to explain?"

"I'm not sure. He was rather cryptic about it."

"And the thing he wanted to show you?"

"He didn't say what it was."

Detective Bailey was a serious-faced man with dark hair, a five 'oclock shadow, and thin lines etched between his eyebrows as if he spent most of his time frowning. He struck her as calm and methodical, the kind of practical person who didn't have a lot of flights of fancy or flashes of inspiration, but still got to the truth eventually.

He asked her questions about the emails that Reed had sent her, how the two of them had met, the nature of their friendship, what time she had expected him, his habits (as far as she knew them), and so on.

"What...where was he?" she asked.

Detective Bailey stood up, puffing air out of his cheeks. "I will answer your questions, Ms. Prouty, but first I have to ask. Would you come with me to identify the body? Do you think you can do that?"

She shuddered. The thought of seeing Reed lying there, dead, did not appeal. But then...who else did he have on the island? He was such a solitary, private man. Who else did he have anywhere?

∼

Detective Baily drove her to the Nantucket Funeral Home, a bright new manufactured building with white fiber cement siding and a new white sign in the brightly lit parking lot. On the island, any building that wasn't covered with gray shingles stood out. The Nantucket Cottage Hospital, which was where the morgue was usually located, was in the middle of changing locations from several different buildings in town to the new building on Prospect Street, and apparently the morgue hadn't made it yet.

It wasn't like a morgue in horror movies: claustrophobic and shadowed, with flickering fluorescent lights overhead. It felt like being in someone's house and going downstairs to the basement. She half-expected a large screen TV and a big couch. In the first room she entered, there was a rocking chair with a small monitor in front of it, a small stack of thin cloths, a child's playpen, and a box full of toddler-safe toys.

The detective led her through a pair of double doors to a sterile-looking area, a viewing room of sorts. It held a single occupied gurney covered with a sheet. She wouldn't have to go into the autopsy room, thank goodness. A mortician waited for them.

She sniffled. Detective Bailey said, "Ms. Prouty? Do you need a glass of water?"

"No, I'll be fine."

She and Detective Bailey stood next to the gurney as the mortician took the far edge of the sheet in both gloved hands, then looked at her. Part of Angie's brain was gibbering *I can't do this, I can't do this!* but she ignored it. This already felt worse than finding Alexander Snuock's body on the floor of his house last July, and she hadn't even seen Reed yet. Maybe it was all the build-up. Maybe it was the fact that she actually *liked* Reed. Either way, she needed to pull herself together. She was strong, and the events of last summer had hardened her. She could do this.

"Ready?"

She nodded.

The sheet was withdrawn and Angie took a step backward. Detective Bailey grabbed her arm—not to keep her from running away, but to make sure she didn't stumble.

"You okay?"

"That's Reed," she said. His skin was strangely pale, even though he'd been a swarthy man. Death made his skin look wrong. The backs of his shoulders were red, she noticed. There was a large bruise on his forehead, swollen and red with blood. His eyes and mouth were closed.

"What happened?" she said.

"That is Reed Edgerton?" Detective Baily said.

"Yes, that is Reed Edgerton."

"Are you certain?"

"I am certain," she said, swallowing hard. "What happened, Detective Bailey?"

"Thank you, Pam, you can cover him back up," Detective Bailey said to the mortician. "I'll tell you, but let's get out of here, shall we?"

"It won't be any easier to take," Angie said.

"It won't be easy," Detective Bailey agreed. "But it can get lots harder. Let's get out of this basement and into the air at least."

The two of them walked out the back door and along the rear drive leading to the street. It wasn't quite cold enough to freeze, but a mist was still coming down, coating everything with a sheen of wetness. It felt like if the air got one degree colder, everything would freeze. Winter was toying with the island, promising bad weather but refusing to give any hint of when.

Detective Bailey turned the corner and suddenly they were walking alongside the park. Throughout the park, bare branches on a scattering of trees had been decorated with LED Christmas lights, and they made the misty air turn a little brighter.

"What we know," Detective Bailey said, "is that Mr. Edgerton was discovered just off Children's Beach. He was found in the water, following the current along the beach. As far as we could tell, he was headed toward Brant Point Light. He was found at one twenty-one a.m., and although we can't get an official time of death until the county coroner comes over on the first ferry, the folks over at the funeral home all say that it looks like he died at least a couple of hours before that."

"How did he die?"

"You saw that bruise," he said.

She nodded.

"Well, they're saying that it could be the bruise or it could be drowning or it could be a combination of both. I'm sure the coroner will be able to sort it out."

"Was he murdered?"

"We can't say at this time. It's a slippery night. Sure looks like it's possible that he slipped and hit his head. No way of saying at this point. You're sure you didn't see him earlier today?"

"I wish I had," she said, "but no."

He gave her a sympathetic look. "It's a hard thing. One second they're there, and the next they're not. There's no shame in feeling torn up about it, even if you weren't that close."

"Thank you. What else can you tell me?"

"Not much. We're trying to find out when he came across on the ferry, but some folks aren't as quick to answer the phone at o'dark thirty in the morning as you are. But we'll find out in the morning, I'm sure. Everyone has to register their names."

Angie's mouth dropped open. "Of course. Registering. Have you had a chance to check with the Chamber of Commerce yet? He was cryptic about his reasons for being here, but I'm sure he would have at least registered for the treasure hunt. He might have signed in there."

"That's true."

"If he did, then at least you'd have the time he registered."

"That'll be my next stop."

The detective walked her back to the funeral home parking lot before taking her to her car. As he dropped her off, he said, "Go home and get some sleep, Angie. We'll try not to disturb you too much tomorrow, but I'm sure it's going to be a tiring day. You remember the questions that I had to ask you when Mr. Snuock passed in July. We'll have to go over everything all over again, in even more detail."

"I remember," she said.

"And I know you're going to be curious, but please don't follow me to the Chamber building. Those folks have had a rough time this last week or so, trying to keep up with the tourists coming in."

"Their coffee maker *and* their registration computer went down," she said.

"At their wit's end," Detective Bailey said. "And that was before one of the tourists died. I guess they're past their wit's end by now."

Chapter 7

ON THE HUNT

When Angie walked through the back door, Aunt Margery was waiting for her with a hug and some cocoa. That brought tears to her eyes all over again. It was stupid. She didn't even know who Reed's nearest family member was. Would they travel to the island for the body, or just have it shipped to the mainland? Would anyone contact her about the funeral? Would she even be invited?

She wasn't going to be able to say goodbye. Or thank you. Or anything else she needed to say.

"Was it an accident?" Aunt Margery asked.

Angie had somehow been transported from the kitchen door to the living room, where she was now wrapped up in an old quilt.

"They don't know yet. But he had a terrible bruise on his forehead. He could have slipped and fallen."

"Do you think that's what happened?"

"I just don't know, Aunt Margery. Part of me wants to think, 'oh, this was clearly a murder case,' so I have an excuse to track down someone and pin the blame on them. But I think what I really want are answers. You hear people say that, you know? 'I just want to know what happened.' But it's true. That's really all I want right now."

Aunt Margery said, "I know what you mean."

"We're nosy, that's what you mean."

"That, too." She leaned back in her calico-covered armchair and sipped some tea. "I know this is the last thing on your mind right now, but what do you think Reed was going to tell you? Maybe he had a clue about the painting?"

"I really don't know. He mentioned something about imposters, but I'm not sure what that means. I just can't believe he's really gone."

"You said he was an art history professor. If there's one thing a historian hates, it's not knowing what really happened. I wonder if he found some historical inaccuracies in the Chamber of Commerce's information about the painting."

"Historians are nosy," Angie said, a small smile stealing across her face as she remembered her many conversations with Reed, "and a factual inaccuracy would be too much for him to bear. It's possible."

"That's why the two of you got along so well together," Aunt Margery said, "both nosy, and both focused on the facts."

"You've never met him."

"And yet I've heard all your stories," she pointed out. "I feel like I know him, at least a little."

Opening the bookstore the next morning was harder than she had expected. Not only was she sleep-deprived, but her grief exhausted her. She had trouble keeping her eyes open.

Of course the gossip had already made the rounds by the time she unlocked the front door and let her early-morning gentlemen in. She could feel their eyes on her, as if probing for answers that she didn't have. They *did* ask her if she was indeed Reed's friend. She oversimplified and said "yes."

And drank a lot of coffee.

Jo stopped by and watched the front of the store for half an hour while Angie took a 20-minute power nap to refresh herself. On waking she looked around the stock area. The shelves in the back were heavy-gauge wire soldered onto sturdy frames, and they were crowded with cardboard boxes and mail bins full of books. The books were all new—she didn't take used books yet. If she had, this room would be twice as packed and she'd have to hire another assistant just to handle buying books. She did hope to expand into buying and selling used books someday, though. It would be a way to help recycle the books around the island. Her heart skipped a beat every time she saw anything even remotely resembling a book in the trash. It was like seeing an abandoned corpse.

She got up and splashed water on her face.

As she looked in the mirror, she saw black circles under her eyes. She'd promised herself that she'd never get involved in another murder mystery again. *No more murders.* She'd told herself she didn't have time to deal with anything like that.

But if she didn't, who would?

The police, obviously. But she just couldn't help but feel like

Detective Baily, who was only five years older than she was, would have the experience to solve the case. Generally deaths on the island involved tourists doing something stupid. Say the coroner did decide that Reed's death had been a murder. What then? They would comb the area for witnesses who had been watching Children's Beach at eleven p.m. or so on a cold, wet night.

So, nobody.

And the body...and *Reed* might not have been dropped into the water anywhere near Children's Beach. It could have been anywhere up-current along the harbor. He could have been out along the wharves talking to someone, or on a boat even.

Detective Bailey would be thorough. He would ask everyone. He would make sure that everyone had an alibi, and that their stories all matched up.

He would do the boring work that was always taken for granted.

Angie was gripping the sides of the sink as tightly as she could. Good grief, what was she thinking? That Detective Bailey, who seemed to have the investigation well in hand, was too stupid to figure out who the murderer was? Or that it even *was* a murder?

Come to think of it, why was she so sure that it was a murder? Just a little while ago, she'd been mostly convinced that it was an accident.

The missing clue, she realized. Reed had wanted to tell her something over dinner. Something about imposters, something about documents...She would never be able to talk to Reed again, but maybe she could find the documents he spoke of in his email. He could have just dropped them into the water—that is, if he'd been walking along one of the wharves with them held in his hand, dangling over the water like a complete idiot.

Which Reed was *not*.

He would have been carrying it in that soft-sided briefcase that he almost always had with him, on a strap over his shoulder.

The bag *might* have slipped over his head and into the water. But Detective Baily had said that he had still had his wallet—that's how they had known his name in the first place. But not the bag. And what about his phone?

She called the police station from inside the bathroom and left a message for Detective Bailey to call her when he had a chance. She didn't want to be suspicious of everything and everyone, and yet a chill was spreading through her. She'd slipped into analyst mode: Where were the holes? What could she take advantage of? Who were her competitors?

She left the back room and thanked Jo, who gave her a sidelong look. She leaned in close and murmured in Angie's ear. "It was murder, wasn't it?"

Angie pressed her lips together and didn't answer. She didn't need to. Jo read the look on her face.

"Lips zipped," she said.

"Don't say anything to anyone about the attic," Angie said.

Jo's pressed her mouth into a thin line. She nodded and left.

Angie put on a mask of good cheer and served her customers, but her mind was racing all the while. Reed's murder was related to the treasure hunt. She was sure of that much. If the mystery were easy to solve, Detective Bailey would solve it. At the very least, he would burn through the thousand and one questions to be asked faster than she could. But if the slow-moving machine of police procedure wasn't enough, she could fill in the gaps with her own investigations. She would leave Detective Bailey alone to handle the methodical, straightforward angle, and she would tackle the mystery from a different direction.

She would come at it from the treasure-hunting angle. Maybe Reed hadn't come to the island specifically for the treasure hunt, but his "quest" must have been related to it, at least.

Find the painting, work backward to Reed's clue, find out who would be hurt by that clue becoming public, and voila, one murderer, served up on a platter.

It all seemed so simple.

Captain Parfait came out of hiding and started inspecting her regulars, who were all surprised but delighted. He ignored their attempts to pet him and stalked the store as though he were pursuing mice. Sometimes he even dropped into a crouch and rocked his hindquarters back and forth as if he were just about to pounce.

The humans in the building couldn't sense that anything had changed, but Captain Parfait could tell.

She was going on the hunt.

∼

Marlee Ingersoll stopped by with Angie's coffee pots at about seven. "They're out again," she said.

"No replacement coffee maker?"

"They're bringing one over on the twelve o'clock Steamship Express. But they can't buy it until the stores open, and then they have to drive to the ferry, and then it has to come over on the ferry, and by then everyone will be insane."

Angie couldn't disagree with her.

"Getting more coffee is not a problem," she said firmly. "How is everyone this morning?"

"Jasper *still* hasn't fixed the computer this morning. He was up all night working on it."

"Poor Jasper."

"He was really mad this morning, too. Apparently the police interrupted him, because they..." her voice dropped into a whisper, "...*found that body in the harbor last night, did you hear?*"

"Yes," Angie said. It was a sign of how overburdened the staff was at the Chamber of Commerce that they didn't know of Angie's friendship with Reed yet. She probably should have said something, but she just couldn't.

"It was terrible," Marlee said, sounding as if she found it all more exciting than otherwise. "The man probably just fell off one of the boardwalks and drowned. I don't know why they had to talk to us. They talked to everyone else this morning, as if they were trying to imply that someone killed him. I live on the west side of the island with my parents, so I'm in the clear. Carol was on the phone with her friend from Boston," Marlee waggled her eyebrows, "and they can check the phone records on that, and Tabitha went to the Shuckery. She *said* she saw you there, too, so I guess you're off the hook, too."

Angie sent her off with two fresh pots of coffee, thinking hard.

After Marlee left, more tourists started coming in. It was still slower than it had been on Monday or Tuesday, but busier than Wednesday had been.

At eight-thirty, the fellowship of retired gentlemen finished their coffee, newspapers, and gossip, and decided to move along to bigger and better things—coffee, cards, dominoes, and *more* gossip. She told them all to be careful outside. The mist had continued throughout the night without freezing, but the temperature was forecasted to drop throughout the day. After sunset, the wind was supposed to pick up considerably, and if the mist continued, the islanders could be looking at icy roads, downed powerlines, and collapsed branches tomorrow morning.

Her gentlemen all took daily walks, even in the worst weather. She lived in fear that one of them was going to break a hip or something on their way to or from the bookstore.

Walter called soon afterward. He was aware of her customers' habits and knew just when the store was most likely to experience a lull.

"I heard," he said without preamble.

"Oh, Walter. I'm so glad you called."

"I can't believe you opened the store today."

"I had to. I have customers and employees who depend on me.

"Are you doing all right?"

"For the most part? I guess I am. I'm tired, though."

"Of course you're tired, Angie," he said. "A friend just died and you barely got any sleep last night. Plus the shock and grief take a toll. I remember when Dad died. I was walking around so exhausted all the time."

Angie felt a rush of affection surge through her. It felt good to have Walter's support.

"What happened?" Walter asked.

"He seems to have slipped and fallen," Angie said.

"Did the police say that?"

"They said they were investigating."

"So they're treating it as suspicious."

Angie looked around the store. There were only a handful of customers milling around at the moment, and none of them seemed to need assistance. She leaned against the espresso machine counter and said, "I can tell you something and you'll be discreet about it, right?"

"Absolutely."

She told him about Reed's plans to come to the island, meet her for supper, and share some documents with her, and explain his mysterious quest. She described how careful and considerate Reed had been, and how unlike him it would be to willingly stand her up without contacting her. She explained the absence of Reed's briefcase, despite the presence of his wallet, and noted how strange it would have been for him to lose or leave behind an item he had promised to show her.

"Hm," Walter said. "That makes me wonder."

"What?"

"Why he didn't call you earlier, if he died at eleven p.m."

She had no answer for that.

After a pause, Walter said, "I know this is hard, Angie. I'll be back soon."

"When?"

"In time for the gala. I hope late tonight or early tomorrow morning. I'll call when I get on the ferry."

∽

She had completely forgotten about the gala, which was to be held at the Whaling Museum on Friday night. The museum was the centerpiece of the Nantucket Historical Association. In addition to its usual array of exhibits, including the full-sized sperm whale skeleton hanging in the main gallery, the building was currently well-decorated with Christmas trees sponsored by local businesses.

Angie and the twins had discussed sponsoring a joint tree, but hadn't been able to get the approval they needed for Mickey's ideas, which involved a lot of frosting on styrofoam shapes as ornaments. The tree that Angie and Aunt Margery had at home was decorated with several sugar egg ornaments that had been in the family for over fifty years, so Angie hadn't seen a problem with the frosting idea. But the association had made a valid point: the last thing they needed at the museum was mice.

Angie had taken the opportunity to set up a holiday-themed book tree, with huge coffee table books at the bottom, cookbooks in the center, novels above that, and kids' board books at the top. She arranged a few strings of white LED lights around the tree, and added an angel on top. The angel's harp had been removed and replaced with a miniature copy of *Pride and Prejudice* and a teensy pair of wire eyeglasses had been placed on her nose. The bookworm angel. Back at the store, she'd changed her "bestseller" rack over to a "Found on the Whaling Museum Book Tree!" rack. Done and done.

She wasn't involved in preparations for the gala, thank goodness. The bakery would provide sweets, Sheldon would handle the cash bar, and Aunt Margery had written most of the souvenir program, but Angie's contribution began and ended with the book tree.

Still, that really wasn't much of an excuse for completely forgetting it.

She had already picked out a dress and a backup dress, tried them both on, and decided that she could live with the fact that she wasn't the pencil-legged waif of her high school years. She had also planned out her hairstyle and makeup for the evening and done a test run of both. In short, she had generally overthought every possible aspect of appearing in public with Walter.

He'd be back tonight or early tomorrow morning.

Angie's thoughts turned back to the conversation they had just had. Like Walter had said, why hadn't Reed called her earlier if he hadn't died until eleven p.m.?

A pair of customers bustled through the door. As she drew closer, she realized they were the Beauchamps. Angie greeted them warmly, still sticking to her policy of pretending that she had somehow missed the disturbing conversation they'd had the previous morning. She prepared their usual orders—coffee with lots of cream and sugar for him, and plain black for her.

"Any pastries?" she asked.

Mrs. Beauchamp gave her a broad smile. "No."

"Yes," said Mr. Beauchamp. "You need to eat."

"I don't need to eat pastry." Mrs. Beauchamp turned to Angie, her face a mask of embarrassment. "No offense."

"None taken," she said.

"You didn't eat anything at all this morning at the hotel."

"I'm not hungry."

"If you pass out from low blood sugar, you have only yourself to blame."

Mrs. Beauchamp turned to Angie. "I do *not* have diabetes. Charles, please stop confusing this young lady and pay the bill."

"Even if *you're* not having a pastry, *I* am," he announced. "That one."

He jabbed a finger toward the glass. Angie got the sense that his selection had nothing to do with what he liked or didn't like. He had chosen the biggest pastry in the case, a large twisted Danish with orange peel and cardamom icing.

They both watched Angie put the Danish on a plate, then put it in the toaster oven to heat. Mrs. Beauchamp licked her lips. Angie cleaned the countertops behind her as she waited for the pastry, sure that the two retirees were giving each other challenging looks behind her back.

When the timer went off, Angie pulled the pastry out and put it on the glass countertop of the bakery case.

"Would you like anything else?" she said politely.

Mr. Beauchamp pulled a twenty-dollar bill out of his wallet and tapped the long edge on the glass. "I don't know," he said to his wife. "Would *you* like anything else? Because I'm not going to let you pick at my pastry whenever my head is turned. Either get your own pastry or keep your hands off mine."

"I'm fine," Mrs. Beauchamp insisted, her eyes still fixed on the pastry.

Angie rang them up, and they walked over to the comfy chairs in the café area. Mrs. Beauchamp picked up one of the used books Angie kept stocked on the tables. Most of them were from her own collection, or from a bargain bin somewhere. They were popular titles that customers could take home with them for a dollar or two in the small donation cup on a nearby shelf. And if a dollar or a book walked off with one of her retired gentlemen who was struggling, so be it.

She watched the couple for a moment. She wouldn't exactly say there was tension between the two of them, but they were giving each other funny looks. On her next tour around the bookstore to see if anyone needed any help, she stopped to see if they were having any luck with the treasure hunt.

"The treasure hunt?" Mrs. Beauchamps said, looking nervously toward the back of the store. "No new developments."

Angie followed her gaze, but saw nothing out of the ordinary.

"That's too bad," she said. "Are you planning to come to the treasure hunt gala on Friday? It starts at five-thirty at the Whaling Museum."

"That museum has a damned big whale hanging from the ceiling," Mr. Beauchamp said. "We've been in. Seen all the Christmas trees and everything. No need to go again, unless there's an open bar."

"No, it's a cash bar."

"Then I think we'll give it a miss," Mr. Beauchamp said, giving his wife an almost stern look.

Mrs. Beauchamp's face was beet red—so red, in fact, that Angie was worried about her.

"Are you all right?" Angie asked.

Mrs. Beauchamp coughed into her hand, rather vigorously, then reached out and took a napkin.

Mr. Beauchamp slapped the leg of his trousers. "Had to steal a piece, didn't you? And then you choked on it! That's just what you deserve."

Mrs. Beauchamp took a gasping breath, then stood up and walked to the public toilet at the back of the store, while Mr. Beauchamp continued chuckling to himself.

Angie beat a hasty retreat back to the café counter. Once again, the Beauchamps had thrown her for a loop.

In between customers, she managed to do a little research on the computer at the sales desk. She was able to track down a list of properties owned by the Snuock family around the turn of the century, which was a little earlier than she wanted, but it did include the building containing both the bookstore and the bakery. She printed out a map of the island, then started plotting out roughly where the properties were and labeling their current business names and property owners. At a glance, the Snuocks had been a wealthy family even then, but their property ownership hadn't reached its current extent.

After a few minutes, she tore herself away from the map and did another circuit of the store.

The destructive archaeology student, Alayna Karner, had returned, sneaking into the store without attracting Angie's notice. This time she was staring at the angle of the roof as it met the bookshelves in the rear of the store.

"Can I help you?" Angie asked, thinking, *Honestly, I'm not sure I can.*

"Have you done any additional research on the ownership of your building? Is there an attic access? Can I access it?"

"Yes, but not much; yes, but not from the bookstore; if you don't mind rat poison lying around and you ask for permission," Angie said.

"Where is it?"

Angie sighed and wrote the name of the building manager on the back of one of her business cards, then handed it to the woman. "You should run it by the Chamber of Commerce if you're really interested in looking up there."

"I've been to their office. Twice. They're always busy."

Angie couldn't deny that was probably going to be the case for a while. "Well, call the property manager anyway."

"Have you been up there?"

"No, but I've seen the access panel. Unless you can pick locks and climb bare walls, you're going to need some assistance."

"I'll call him," the woman promised. "Thank you for your help."

"Can I help you with anything else?"

"A cup of coffee?"

Angie left Alayna Karner in the café area paging through one of the used books—a copy of Victor Hugo's *The Man Who Laughs*. An unexpected choice, but Angie had long since learned that you can't judge a book by the readers who pick it up.

The back door jingled, and Angie glanced at it over her shoulder. Aunt Margery had arrived early, which reminded Angie that nobody from the Chamber of Commerce had come over for coffee lately.

She called the office. This time, the person who answered the phone was Carol Brightwell, the executive director. She thanked Angie effusively for the coffee she'd delivered, then asked her to bring more over. "Just one this time," she said.

"It hasn't been busy today?"

"No, it has. But the new coffee machine is on its way over on the ferry. We should be fine."

Angie filled up two pots—just in case—and left the store in Aunt Margery's capable hands.

Chapter 8

EXILES & DISCOVERIES

The Chamber of Commerce wasn't merely less hectic than it had been previously. It felt hushed. The tourists who were looking at the displays and maps and reading fliers from the rack seemed to tiptoe around the room. Their voices didn't rise above a whisper.

After the chaos of the previous day, it was probably for the best.

At first Angie couldn't figure out why, but then she noticed that the lights hadn't been brightened for the day—they were still on some kind of dim setting—and the room felt dark and heavy, as though a storm were rolling in.

Marlee Ingersoll was watching the front desk. When she glanced up and saw Angie, she jumped up and walked over to help with the big coffee pots, but did so on tiptoe.

"Hi!" she whispered. "Coffee! I'm glad to see you."

"Isn't the new coffee maker coming over on the ferry?"

"But what if it's delayed?" Marlee hissed. "Or...worse? What if it gets here and everyone starts to argue over how to set it up? It could be hours!"

Angie snorted softly through her nose. The quiet was getting to her, too.

The two of them carried the coffee pots to the break room. Angie picked up the empties and closed the door softly behind her.

"Just so you know," Marlee said, "Carol's thinking of saying something at the gala—giving you a thank you card or something."

"Thanks for the heads' up," Angie said.

"I think she's going to be passing out a lot of cards this year," Marlee added. "Did you hear about Jasper?"

"No, what happened?"

"He had some kind of heart palpitation thing and had to go to the hospital this morning while I was talking to you!"

"Oh, no, is he all right?"

"He's been moved out of critical care and into his own room, so I think he is."

"I should visit him," Angie said.

"*Don't* bring him any coffee," Marlee whispered. "The doctor says that he was drinking energy drinks *and* coffee *and* taking NoDoz at the same time. He could have had a heart attack. So now he has to cut back."

"Poor Jasper," Angie said. "He's probably going through coffee withdrawal right now."

"That's the worst," Marlee agreed.

"Marlee, about Reed Edgerton's accident yesterday..." Angie began.

"Oh, man. I heard that you were his friend. I'm so sorry that I was a jerk this morning. I had no idea. I'm so sorry."

"It's okay," Angie said. "But I wanted to know if he had ever come through here."

"Nope," Marlee said. "I had to go through all the paperwork Jasper entered and check everything over. When he entered it, he added a ton of mistakes. There were even a couple I had to delete and start over with. He put stuff in like 'Vincent Van Gogh' in some of the entries, swapped people's addresses, even wrote some of the numbers in backward. But anyway I had to check all his entries from yesterday and compare them to the slips so I know for sure that Mr. Edgerton never checked in with us."

"When did the computer come back up?" Angie said.

"The software stopped erasing entries and rebooting, I don't know, around eight a.m.," Marlee said. "Why?"

"Did a woman by the last name of Karner come in and ask you about searching my building's attic sometime today?"

"I don't think so? I don't remember anyone asking about your attic, but it's been a weird day."

"Did she register yesterday?"

"I'm not sure." Marlee sat down in front of the desk, woke up the computer, and started typing. "Karner with a C?"

"I think it's Karner with a K."

"Um... yes, here we are," Marlee said. "We do have a Karner with a K registered. What was her first name?"

"Alayna."

"A-L-A-Y-N-A?" she spelled out.

"I'm not sure, honestly."

Marlee pressed the arrow keys several times. "Well, that's the only Alayna Karner we have registered."

"Then that must be her. Thanks."

"No problem. Everybody here owes you one, anyway."

"Don't worry about it."

"I take my favors seriously," Marlee said, her eyebrows pinching together.

"Okay, okay," Angie laughed. "The next time I need an alibi during a murder case, I'll call you."

"Friends help you move," Marlee said. "Real friends help you move bodies."

Angie had heard the line a hundred times but she laughed anyway. Sometimes timing trumped originality.

∽

Out on the street, she hesitated. The new hospital building wasn't too far to walk, but she was carrying a pair of coffee pots. They weren't heavy, but they also probably weren't the best "get well" gift to bring along on a visit to someone constrained from drinking coffee.

She walked back to the bookstore, dropped off the pots, and asked her great-aunt if she'd mind if Angie took an hour or two to visit Jasper at the hospital.

Aunt Margery said, "It should be fine. You need to stop working so much. Have you read anything today?"

Angie laughed. "Reading isn't like brushing your teeth, Aunt Margery. If you skip it for a day or two, you'll still be fine. I promise."

"Did you?"

"No."

"Then take a book with you. Go home and take a nap while you're at it."

Angie yawned before she could stop herself. She thought about arguing that she was fine, but changed her mind. She'd already lost that argument the day before—she couldn't do it all herself.

So instead she laughed at herself and said, "You know, I had completely forgotten that the gala was coming up tomorrow."

"Tomorrow!" Aunt Margery said. "Gadzooks, are you joking? What day is it? It's only Wednesday."

"Wednesday was yesterday."

"My mind is going, isn't it?"

"'All children, except one, grow up.'"

"Too easy. Peter Pan."

"I just like the sound of it," Angie said.

She was summarily shooed out of the bookstore, although on her way out she did remind Aunt Margery that Janet was working on a list of information she would need from Angie before putting together a marketing plan.

The door closed behind her with a jingle. Then Angie turned

suddenly and knocked on it, moaning, "Let me in, let me in," until Aunt Margery, who hadn't actually locked the door, let her in again.

"What is it, you cat? In or out?"

"I forgot my book. And I thought I'd bring something for Jasper."

"You may come back in," Aunt Margery said, "but if you're still here in ten minutes I shall toss you back out again."

∼

The new hospital building was nice. It managed to look modern and professional without standing out too much. The cement siding was the same shade of gray as the worn shingles that could be seen all over town, and it was trimmed with white. There was an orange ramp leading up to the front door.

She had no idea what kind of books Jasper liked to read, so she brought him three: a recent Jack Reacher novel, a history of the Impressionists (more in memory of Reed than anything else), and a silly bodice-ripper romance by Tessa Dare that was packed with silk dresses and goofy hidden references to popular culture. Why not?

"You have a visitor," the nurse said as she knocked on the frame of Jasper's door.

"Come in," his voice called, a little hoarse.

He was sitting up in bed with his glasses on. His skin looked gray, almost wooden, and Angie couldn't keep her concern from showing on her face.

"Hi," she said. "How are you feeling?"

"They say I might be able to go home tomorrow," he said dejectedly, "as long as I let myself rest and don't go back to work. But I don't see how that's supposed to happen. As soon as I cross the threshold, they'll find me. It'll be just one little thing after another until I'm back to working sixteen-hour days."

Angie said, "I'd tell you to just take it easy, but that would be the pot calling the kettle black."

"Have they found the painting yet?" Jasper asked cautiously. "It would all be over if someone finds the painting. Mostly over, at least."

She laughed, then schooled her features into a more sympathetic expression. "No, nobody's made any significant progress. Otherwise I would have heard about it."

"I'm sorry to hear about your friend."

She deflated, her shoulders falling and her head bowing. The books she had brought suddenly felt unbearably heavy, so she set them down onto his swing table. "Thank you," she murmured. "I didn't know him terribly well, but it just came as such a shock. And the thing is, I knew instinctively that something was wrong as soon as..." She was about to spit out, "as soon as I called your office and he hadn't registered yet," but then she paused. The unspoken words surprised her, and she wasn't sure why. She cleared her throat. "Well, the minute he was late for dinner at Sheldon's. He's always early."

"Do they know what happened to him?"

"He fell and hit his head," Angie said. There was something else she wasn't ready to talk about—her suspicions that it was murder. That would just remind him of her history with the Alexander Snuock murder case, which every nosy nelly on the island wanted her to talk about in great, lengthy, tiresome, and embarrassing detail. "For some reason, he came over to the island to do something that might be related to the treasure hunt, never showed up at the Chamber of Commerce, missed our supper without contacting me, and then ended up in the harbor."

Jasper frowned. "Did he know anyone else on the island besides you? It almost sounds like he came over here on, er, well, personal business that you didn't know anything about."

"Personal business?" Angie asked. "I hadn't thought about it. He might have? He never mentioned anything like that to me, but then he never mentioned anything about his personal life. I suppose I might have been briefly introduced to some of his colleagues in Boston at art shows, but...surely he would have thought to text me to cancel our plans."

"I'm no detective," Jasper said gently, "but if he came here for personal reasons, maybe it didn't have anything to do with the treasure hunt. Maybe he came chasing a woman, and just had an unfortunate fall. Love will make you do crazy things."

"Love is crazy, I know what you mean."

"Because of Walter."

"Oh, no," she said, "Walter has been a perfect gentleman. I was thinking of the first time I really fell in love. My ex and I lost track of everything, it seemed like. There were friends I didn't speak to for over three years, and I barely noticed I hadn't, until we broke up again."

Jasper's frown deepened. "Your ex wasn't abusive, was he?"

"No," Angie said. "He cheated on me and stole my ideas at work, though."

"They say good artists copy, and great artists steal. I suppose that doesn't apply here, though. Sorry about your ex Angie, he sounds terrible."

"Yeah he was. Talk about bad memories." Angie said, sitting down in the chair beside the bed. "I take it you've had bad experiences in the past, too."

His lips twitched. "Ex-wife."

Angie thought about Walter, and how she wanted him to come back to the island, but she also thought about how formal and genteel they both kept things when he was here. Maybe he'd had problems, too. She barely knew anything about his past love life. She just knew he was currently single. Other than his relationship with her, of course, but she wasn't really sure what that amounted to.

She shook her head. In fact, now that she was thinking about it, a past trauma might explain Reed's behavior, too—that tendency he'd had of holding others at arm's length.

"That's definitely something to think about," she said. "Not just about Doug, my ex, that is. I mean about Reed. He always kept himself a little aloof from other people, even though he was a charming man."

"It's hard to trust again after a bad relationship," Jasper said.

"Why do people screw each other over like that?" she asked. Then answered her own question, because she remembered Doug's attitude about their break-up. "Because they can. Because they need someone to love them unconditionally, and they don't know how to love someone back."

"That sounds about right," Jasper agreed.

Angie caught herself wondering about those two mysterious lovers in the past, Victor Nouges and…who? Who had he given the painting to?

Even if their romance had been illicit, she was sure that their emotions had been real. You didn't give a Monet painting to someone who didn't have your deepest admiration and respect. Not even back then, when they weren't worth millions of dollars.

Jasper took all three books, admitting that he'd never read a romance or a Jack Reacher novel before. His tastes ran towards literary fiction and historical non-fiction. He was a James Joyce fan specifically. She made a mental note and said, "You look too tired for James Joyce."

"My thoughts feel like one of the longer Molly Bloom passages," he admitted. "One long sentence running around nowhere most of the time."

She laughed, wished him some peace and quiet, and told him to call her if he wanted more books.

On the way out of the hospital, she got a text from Aunt Margery asking her to pick up some cream and a few other things for the afternoon rush. "No hurry to come back," the message added. Angie rolled her eyes. All right, she got the hint—find something to do for a couple of hours.

Janet knew how to ring people up and record purchases on the computer so they adjusted inventory, but Angie had really only shown her what she had to know in order to survive working the café counter. "Give Janet more training on the computer if things get slow," she texted back to Aunt Margery. "I'm going to pick up lunch somewhere. Want anything?"

"Will do, have fun, I'm good," Aunt Margery texted back.

So...now what?

It was a little scary that Angie didn't know what to do with herself now that she wasn't trapped at the store. She walked back to her car slowly, almost suspiciously. It felt like she was waiting for the other shoe to drop.

She climbed into the car and noticed more books on the back seat, ones that she'd picked up without thinking about it on her way to Sheldon's the other night.

The books that Reed had ordered. She hadn't shipped them yet, thinking that he'd find them more useful while he was on the island looking for treasure rather than back in Boston where he couldn't get them.

A lump rose in her throat.

All right. This was the plan: she was going to get something to eat from one of the small cafés near the harbor, bundle up, and go out to read for a while by the water.

She picked up a hot baked turkey sandwich with cranberry relish and blue cheese, bought a cup of hot cocoa, and walked out along the wharf until she found a seat on a sunny, sheltered bench. One of the books from Reed's order had sounded familiar, so she'd grabbed it. *A Light in the Dark: Putting a Value on the Brant Point Lighthouse, 1746-1901*, by James A. Higley, Jr. After a few moments, she worked out where she'd heard the title recently—from the list that had been dropped on the floor. She'd tucked the list somewhere for safekeeping in case the customer returned for it. There had been five or six titles, all of them scratched out but the one. She couldn't even begin to remember the others. Maybe she should look.

She ate, staring out at the water and listening for the sounds of boats. But not many people had ventured out on the water in this chilly weather, and since most of the businesses along the wharf were closed up for the season, it seemed she had, ironically, found a place of peace and quiet.

With her legs curled up under her big wool coat, she drank her cocoa and read her book. She let her shadow fall over the page, because otherwise, it was almost too bright out to read.

The history of the Brant Point Lighthouse was what she had expected, more or less. She'd grown up hearing stories about the lighthouse burning down multiple times. Each time she'd heard those stories, she had received the impression that the fires had happened just before she was born, even though they had really happened centuries earlier.

The settlers on the island had been infamously cheap, hence the lighthouse's poor design. And centuries later, Nantucket's natives were still a thrifty lot. Even the wealthiest islanders took pride in managing to scrape along using twenty dollars and a stack of coupons they found on the Internet. They had million-dollar homes and enormous yachts, but they could often be spotted crawling through antique stores looking for a deal. They were born hagglers, and they'd wear a sweater until it unraveled on them before knitting the yarn back up into hats. It was just a part of the local culture, but the fire-prone lighthouse had been an example of thriftiness carried too far.

Had Reed thought the painting was in that little wooden lighthouse at the very end of the point? The most recent incarnation of the structure had been built in 1901, which should make it a possible location for the painting. But the door of the lighthouse was locked to keep the tourists out. Then again, was Reed even looking for the painting?

She looked toward the lighthouse, a squat black and white structure set against a backdrop of sea and sky. A lonely pair of pedestrians was walking along the sand, strolling slowly and enjoying the calm, sunny day.

If she wanted to check the lighthouse for the painting, she'd have to talk to someone at the Chamber of Commerce to get permission and a set of keys. Doing so would probably be a waste of her time. She found it hard to believe that no one had gone over the lighthouse from top to bottom already. If the painting had been somewhere that didn't require dismantling the whole lighthouse, it should have been found long ago. The lighthouse was publicly owned, too, which meant that the mysterious lover wouldn't have been able to access the lighthouse easily over the years. And it would stick out if she had visited it December 17th every year, wouldn't it?

But still, it caught the eye. Maybe Reed had been researching it out of curiosity. It would make sense if he had wanted to learn about historic sites on the island so that he could visit them while he was there.

When her lunch was eaten, her book read, and she'd had enough of a break to satisfy Aunt Margery (hopefully), Angie decided it was time to return to the store. She uncurled herself from the bench, noting that the chill she felt did nothing to curb her restlessness. She followed the wharf back to shore, then started walking along the beach.

She decided not to walk toward Brant Point; the couple out there looked like they were enjoying their solitude. So she turned the other way, losing herself in the bright day, the complete lack of tourists, the feel of sand underfoot, and the whispering of the breeze.

She walked for a while...then paused.

The beach was remarkable for its even texture, with barely a pebble to ruin its purity. But something stood out in the perfect sand. Angie noticed what looked like a small gold piece of metal poking up from the sand.

Her curiosity piqued, she walked over to it shimmering metal. She bent down and saw that the gold was attached to a leather band. Did someone lose their watch?

But it wasn't a watch. It was a briefcase strap with a gold clasp. Angie's throat went tight, she recognized the strap immediately. It was Reed's briefcase. She had seen it many times before, and he was practically never without it. The briefcase was stuck under an impressive amount of sand, nearly completely hidden.

As she pulled the briefcase from under the sand, the cold waves rushed over her ankles and filled her shoes with cold seawater and drenching her socks. She shivered.

She grabbed the strap of the briefcase, threw it over her shoulder—it was light enough that she was pretty sure there was no computer equipment inside—then shook the water from her shoes.

Why was his briefcase down here? It almost looked like someone had hidden it. As she prepared to leave with the briefcase she noticed a reddish brown spot on the sand above the tide line. Was that a blood stain? Angie couldn't be sure, and it was too cold to investigate. She snapped a picture with her phone so she could look at it later.

She climbed back up onto the shore. She was shivering violently now, so it was time to go somewhere warm.

She half-expected someone to rush toward her and demand to know what she was doing, or, worse yet, ask whether she'd found any clues to the location of the painting. But no one stopped her as she walked to Washington Street and made her way back toward the bookstore as swiftly as she could. She'd walked so far along the beach that it would be faster to go straight back on foot than it would be to pick up her car.

The cream would have to wait.

Chapter 9

THE DOCUMENTS IN THE CASE

Aunt Margery looked up as Angie walked through the front door. She stared at the hemlines of Angie's pants, which were waterstained, stiff with salt, and covered in sand. Then she looked at her face. "Are you all right?"

Angie looked around the bookstore. Nobody was at the café counter, and Janet hadn't come in yet.

"Come to the back with me."

Aunt Margery's eyes took in the soft-sided briefcase slung across Angie's shoulder. "Where did you find that? Whose is it?"

"Just come."

Angie led the way to the back of the store, keeping an eye out for treasure hunters along the way. She didn't need an extra nose sniffing around at the moment.

She brought the bag to the inventory table, then hesitated. The bag was covered in sand. She covered the table with one of her gentlemen's used newspapers and set the bag down. She kept her gloves on as she unzipped it.

Inside was a small, cloth-bound book and plastic folder containing a sheaf of papers. The title of the book was *An Old-Fashioned Romance: A Collection of Love Letters from the Eighteenth, Nineteenth, and Early Twentieth Centuries*, edited by Teresa Tukesberry. It was dry and free from water spots or other damage.

She set that aside for the moment, opened the folder, and pulled out the papers.

There were newspaper clippings neatly tucked into a 3 ring binder. Each clipping was in a clear plastic sleeve like Angie used to have in High School. The plastic sleeves had mostly protected the clippings from the water, but a few were water logged.

The clippings were all about forged paintings. Specifically, a forger who was active in Boston many years ago. Each clipping revealed details about the case to catch this forger. The last clipping was from the late 90s and led the reader to believe the case had been dropped.

Opposite the last newspaper clipping was a print out of an email exchange. The email exchange was between Reed and a fine art appraiser.

Professor Edgerton,

Thank you for your inquiry about the recently-discovered copy of Monet's Haystacks at Sunset, 1887. I hope this letter will give you the answers you desire.

The painting, which was purchased by the Boston Museum of Fine Arts two years ago, is an impressive forgery. It required deep analysis to confirm its lack of authenticity. As you suggest in your letters, the style is very similar to the rash of forgeries that appeared in Boston in 1997.

Your suggestion that the artist is in fact the same forger, resurfacing 20 years later, is certainly plausible. But it is, in my opinion, unlikely, for reasons that I will outline below.

Additionally, you claim that the forger likely originated in a New England island town, like Nantucket or Martha's Vineyard, due to the salt water content found on both the recent and past forgeries you mentioned. The chemical compounds found in the paint are consistent with salt water, so your theory is, again, plausible. However, I am not aware of any further evidence connecting the forgeries to a specific location.

In your letter, you suggested that the forger may potentially still be on Nantucket or Martha's Vineyard. You attribute this to a 'hunch.' In my experience as an expert witness in various forgery cases, forgers rarely live in the same place that they work, and even more rarely stay in one place for any period of time. Forgers are typically very intelligent people with great talent, but they are criminals and tend to act like criminals. For more information on this subject, I must direct you to the Boston Police Department, which is investigating the Haystacks *case.*

I hope this response is of some assistance in your personal investigation.

Cordially,

Silvia Rutherford, ISA CAPP

Forensic Art Appraiser

Angie's head swirled with the influx of information. Did Reed think the Monet that everyone was hunting for was a fake? Is that what he meant by impostor?

"Angie," said Aunt Margery, "What is all this?"

"This is Reed's briefcase," Angie replied. "I found it on the beach under some rocks. It looked, well, it looked like someone tried to hide it there."

"Well that would mean he didn't fall, and…"

"And that Reed was murdered, and the murderer hid the briefcase. We need to call Detective Bailey. Now."

∼

Angie took a few moments to sort herself out, then called Detective Bailey, who still hadn't returned her last call. He said, "You moved the briefcase."

"Yes, I did. The tide was coming in and it was going to be washed away."

Detective Bailey sighted. "Okay, don't do anything else. Stay put. I'm on my way."

"Thank you."

Even though the bookstore was perfectly warm and Angie had changed out of her wet socks, she was shivering as if she was standing outside in a blizzard. Aunt Margery handed her a cup of hot cocoa and said, "Drink." She didn't. Instead, she sat in front of the table with her hands curled around the cup and stared blankly at the briefcase.

"How could this have happened?" she asked it. Aunt Margery patted her on the shoulder, then went back to the front of the bookstore.

When Alexander Snuock had been killed, his death had come as a shock and a surprise, but it hadn't felt like an impossibility. Angie's mind had wanted to accept Alexander Snuock's death all too quickly.

He had wronged so many people that it wasn't so much a question of "why" as "who."

Reed was different. Angie's mind rebelled against the reality of the situation. Reed couldn't be dead, not really, because he hadn't done anything to deserve it. It wasn't logical, she knew it, but she couldn't help feeling that way.

After gazing at the briefcase for several minutes, she stood up, grabbed one of the spent, wrinkled newspapers that had been cleared from the café area, and dropped it over the briefcase so that it was completely concealed from view. Strangely, not being able to see the briefcase every second seemed to help break her out of the fugue she had slipped into.

The cocoa had gone cool. It had helped heat her hands, but she had stared into space for so long... She checked the clock. *Twenty minutes.* She had been staring at the briefcase, stuck in a mental loop for the last *twenty minutes.*

And where was Detective Bailey? The police station was only a few minutes' drive from the bookstore, at most.

She walked to the back door of the bookstore and looked out just as someone was approaching it: Tabitha Crispin from the Chamber of Commerce. She opened the door and let Tabitha inside the back of the store.

"Tabitha. Is everything all right?"

"I just wanted to pay you for the coffee," she said.

"Oh!" Angie laughed. She had completely forgotten. "Thank you. I've been keeping track somewhere..." She walked over to the inventory computer and sorted through the dozen or so slips of paper that she'd written notes on to herself, all of them pinned under a glass paperweight. She found the one she needed and led Tabitha into the bookstore.

As they made their way to the front of the store, they chatted about how the treasure hunt was going. Each of them had noticed that the number of tourists on the island seemed to have dropped in the last few days, and they were both curious about the implications. Then, just as Angie was about to sit down at the front desk, Tabitha mentioned a familiar name.

Angie momentarily forgot what she was supposed to be doing at the computer. "I'm sorry, what?" she said. "Could you repeat that?"

"I said, and then of course that terrible Karner woman came in with more of her endless demands."

"I've had to deal with her myself," Angie said. "She tried to pull one of the bookshelves off the wall, can you believe it? She thought there was a secret passage behind it or something."

"Was there?"

"Of course not—only another bookshelf."

They both chuckled over absurdity of it.

Then Tabitha described what Alayna Karner had been up to at the Chamber of Commerce today. Apparently, she wanted permission to tear up the floor at the Brant Point Light House and dig below it for a lockbox. When Tabitha had pointed out that burying the painting under the floor of the lighthouse would have made yearly viewing of it rather awkward, Miss Karner had threatened to call in "some very influential people on this island" to force the Chamber of Commerce to cooperate. When Tabitha had then, reasonably in Angie's opinion, asked to see what kind of proof that Miss Karner had to substantiate her suspicion that the painting was under the floor of the lighthouse,

Miss Karner had refused to provide any. "The second I tell you, you'll tell everyone on the island and word will get out. And then you'll give someone else permission to dig where I want to dig. Because that's how places like this work. You're all completely inbred!"

And then she'd flounced out of the building and marched out of sight down the street.

Angie burst out laughing, loud enough to draw the stares of several people in the bookstore. Tabitha joined her.

Finally, Tabitha let out a breath. "Thank you. I needed a laugh. I have to keep reminding myself that it only *seems* like everything is going badly."

"Oh, me too," Angie said. "We've been so busy that I sometimes find myself bracing for some nebulous disaster that probably won't ever happen. I have a bad habit of micromanaging everything in this store, as if I'm the only person who can be trusted with responsibility. But I'm working on that. And to be honest, it's nice being busy. I just need to adapt and make some adjustments to my management style."

It was Reed's death that had really put things into perspective. Compared to that, any real or imagined problems at the bookshop seemed inconsequential.

Her pain must have shown on her face, because Tabitha clasped her arm firmly. "I'm sorry about your friend. I don't believe I've had a chance to say that yet."

"Thank you." Angie forced herself to keep it together. She had a job to do. "Tabitha, I still haven't managed to...to sort out exactly what happened to him. I keep dwelling on it. I don't know even when he arrived. I have to go to the ferry station later and see if they'll tell me when he came over."

"And you want to know when he checked in with us," Tabitha said. "I'll go check, sweetie, and call you right back."

"Thank you, but Marlee said she didn't remember seeing his name when she entered the registration slips into the computer this morning."

Tabitha hummed in acknowledgment, but she didn't look quite convinced. "I'd better double-check, just to make sure. Marlee typed it all up in a rush after Jasper collapsed this morning, so she might have missed something."

Angie finished ringing up Tabitha for the bill, entered it into the computer, then checked the time again. Half an hour had passed, and Detective Bailey still hadn't arrived. All right, something must have come up. If she hadn't heard from him by the time Tabitha had called back about Reed, then she would call again to remind him to retrieve the briefcase.

In the meanwhile, however, she wanted to go through Reed's papers a little more thoroughly.

She did another lap around the bookstore, checking on customers. Janet had come in at some point and was watching the café counter, and Aunt Margery was discussing something with a customer who held a knitting book in one hand and a cozy mystery in the other. Angie smiled at her and went around the rest of the store.

Still no Detective Bailey.

But Mr. Motorcycle—the man from Indiana who had lost his marriage and job and decided to travel the country—had returned. He was sitting in one of the café chairs and staring out the window. His to-go cup of coffee sat next to him with its lid removed, and a plume of steam curled toward the ceiling.

Angie walked back to the café counter and said to Janet, "Card or cash on that one?" She nodded toward Mr. Motorcycle.

"Debit." Janet reached down into the trash and picked up a curl of paper. He hadn't kept his copy of the receipt.

Mr. Motorcycle's name was apparently Wyatt Gilmore.

"How was he?" Angie asked.

"Fine. He seems down. But he wasn't rude or anything," Janet said.

"Thanks."

Angie checked the back room to see if Detective Bailey had somehow appeared there. No dice.

She made up her mind abruptly and walked over to Wyatt Gilmore. Just a few moments earlier, she had worn the same blank expression that she was seeing on his face now, and she abruptly felt worried for him. Maybe she was just being overdramatic, but it seemed like he was nearing the end of his rope.

She sat in a chair at an angle to his and said, "Nice day out, isn't it?"

He started, looking at her as though she were some kind of ghost.

"It is," he said carefully.

"I can't help but notice that you're staring out the window and letting your coffee get cold," she said. "Is something wrong?"

His eyes widened and he seemed to hunch into himself guiltily. "How did you know?"

"I don't know anything," she said gently. "You just look like you need someone to talk to, and I'm in the mood to listen. I guess I'm feeling a bit paranoid lately. A friend of mine passed recently. He was such a private man…I have so many questions."

"I'm sorry to hear it," Gilmore said politely, but nervously—as if he suspected this conversation were a setup.

"And while I have to admit that I'm genuinely nosy, I also have to admit that I'm a little worried about you. This is the second time you've come in here looking for… I don't know. Something."

She was putting her foot in her mouth, she knew it. He was going to march out of here and not look back—the crazy nosy bookseller could stuff it!

"Desperate," Gilmore said. "That's the look you're seeing. Desperate."

She didn't say anything. Often all you had to do once you got someone talking was shut up.

But not today. Today she and Wyatt Gilmore stared at each other as if they were on either side of the Grand Canyon.

The front door opened, and a tall, loping figure burst through it carrying big white pastry flats. Mickey. He was whistling.

Gilmore gave Mickey's back a ghost of a smile. "That guy," he said.

"What about him?"

"He reminds me of when I was younger."

Angie couldn't see it. They didn't look anything alike, and she hadn't heard a single goofy, off-kilter thing come out of Gilmore's mouth. But she wasn't going to argue with him. "Oh?"

"I played basketball when I was younger. Back before I met my wife, when I was in college."

Smoothly, he transitioned the discussion over to his college years. He had played college basketball for the Hoosiers, and apparently it had been the highlight of his life. Since then, everything had gone downhill.

In the middle of a sentence, he cut himself off and said, "My name is Wyatt. Wyatt Gilmore."

"Angie Prouty."

They shook hands. Wyatt laughed and said, "You must think I'm a complete loser, talking endlessly about my basketball years."

"I think you're going through some hard times right now," Angie said.

"Thank you for listening. I feel better, even if I haven't said a word about what's actually bothering me. But I suppose that's not too hard to guess, from what I told you the first time I came into the bookstore."

She agreed. "You did lay down some pretty big hints."

"I've been turning it over and over in my mind, but I can't find any answers. What to do next? I don't have a clue. It feels like I need to keep riding my motorcycle across the country until…"

"Until what?"

"Just until, I guess. Not a lot of what I think makes any sense."

"Isn't there anywhere that you want to be? Anything you want to do?"

"No," he said.

She wasn't sure she believed him. She'd had friends who had gone completely mental after a breakup before. She had almost turned into one of them herself when she and Doug had split up. But then again, she had always had a home and family to go back to, here on the island.

Suddenly, there was another person sitting on the other side of Wyatt Gilmore. Mickey had swung one lanky leg over a chair and slid into it, bouncing off the thick cushions.

"Looks like a serious conversation," Mickey said. "Time to stop that. How's it going?"

"Rough," Angie admitted.

"I heard," Mickey said. "Jo sends her love and all that, she'll see you later and make sure you're okay. As for me, I'm giving you my sympathy in the best way I know how. With cupcakes."

She laughed. She couldn't help it.

"And you, sir?" Mickey said. "You look like death warmed over."

Wyatt Gilmore gaped at him.

"Let me guess," Mickey said. "Your wife is gone, your farm is gone, someone ran over your dog, and the truck won't start."

"How…?"

"Oh, man. I have a couple of friends from college back on the mainland who are going through a divorce right now. From each other. I could recognize that look a million miles away."

Angie hadn't heard about the friends divorcing—whoever they were—and immediately suspected that Mickey had quickly grilled Janet or Aunt Margery for details while her back was turned. Mickey could be quite the con artist, and in college he had regularly scammed money off bar patrons to pay his tab. In short, he was probably lying.

"Anyway," Mickey said, "I really came to tell you that Jo finally broke down and let me look in the attic of the bakery to see if the painting was up there. Spoiler alert, it wasn't."

"That's too bad," Angie said politely.

"It is, it is," Mickey said. "But probably not such a bad thing. I mean, what if it *had* been up there? I'd have to donate the damn thing to the Chamber of Commerce, in exchange for what? Maybe a stupid party?"

"You could have told me, and then I'd get the prize money," Wyatt said.

"Split it fifty-fifty? No way. Jo would find out for sure, because the first thing I would do would be to buy a new oven for the bakery. I guess other people might notice, too."

"Like the IRS," Angie said.

"There is that," Mickey admitted. "Anyway, no painting, no problem, right?"

"Not from my point of view," Wyatt said.

"Sure, sure. Did your ex take all the money or something?"

"Not really. I just lost my job at the same time."

Mickey took in Wyatt's leathers and the helmet under one arm. "So you're driving across the country just going where the wind takes you? Cool."

"It's terrible," Wyatt admitted. "I worked myself to death…I don't know anyone outside of my job."

"It's just a job," Mickey said. "Throw it away and start over. It's not like you owned the place, is it?"

The two of them started talking about Wyatt's situation in greater depth, both of them going over the details pretty intensely. Angie stood up and started to sidle away. When she was out of Wyatt's sight, she gave Mickey a thumb's up. He rubbed his eye to wink covertly at her.

She walked back to the café area, made herself a cappuccino, and claimed a cupcake with tiny marshmallows on it. Hot chocolate. And, unlike the one Aunt Margery had brought her earlier, it wouldn't go cold in twenty minutes.

Where *was* Detective Bailey?

Angie's phone buzzed in her pocket. "Hello, Pastries and Page-Turners, Angie Prouty speaking. How many I help you?"

"Tabitha from the Chamber of Commerce," Tabitha said. "I double-checked the entries for…well, the person you wanted to know about."

"And?"

"We don't have any records of your friend from yesterday. I'm sorry, Angie."

"I thought not," Angie said with a sigh.

Tabitha paused for a moment, then said, "Do you need me to come back to the bookstore?"

It was very thoughtful of her, but Angie had several good options if she needed a shoulder to cry on, and everyone at the Chamber of Commerce had to be busy. She swallowed. "No, it just hit me hard for a moment. I'll be all right."

"Call me if you need me."

"Thank you, I will. You, too."

"If we all survive the gala this weekend, I just might."

∼

Detective Bailey still hadn't called. Angie found herself back in the stock room, standing in front of the table where she'd stashed the briefcase. Tempting.

Too tempting.

Angie flipped through the other papers in the briefcase. She found more information on famous paintings and forgeries of those paintings. Angie wondered what made Reed so sure that the painting was a forgery. But then, she might have it all wrong. He might not have thought the lost Monet was forged. All she knew for certain was that he was investigating forgeries that had been discovered in Boston.

She pulled out her phone to re-read Reed's email. He mentioned an impostor, Angie had assumed he was referring to a forged painting. But what if he was actually referring to the forger?

She sighed out loud. Without Reed, she couldn't know for sure.

By the time Angie had finished re-reading the email and trying to sort out what it meant, her eyes felt dry and itchy. She called the police station. "Detective Bailey was supposed to stop by earlier," she told the person at the reception desk. "Have you seen him?"

"Is this Angela Prouty speaking?"

"My name is Agatha, but I go by Angie. It's me."

"Then he left you a message. 'Following lead, will try to be there in half an hour. Bailey.'"

"When did he leave the message?"

"About an hour ago."

Her phone beeped.

"I have another call coming in, I think it might be him," Angie said. "Thank you, I'll call back if it isn't."

"Welcome."

She switched to the other call.

"Miss Prouty? Detective Bailey here." His voice sounded excited.

"What is it?"

"Using gloves, wrap up the briefcase in a garbage bag and tape it shut. Then drive down to the location where you found the briefcase. Can you do that?"

"Be there in ten minutes," she promised.

Chapter 10

WHO YOU KNOW

As soon as Angie drove up to the beach with the black trash bag in the back of her little red VW Golf, she realized what Detective Bailey was about to tell her: that if Reed had gone into the water here, it couldn't have been an accident. There were no hard surfaces where he could have struck his head, and no elevated surfaces he could have fallen from. The only exception was a deck attached to an apartment building that overlooked the water at high tide, but public access was blocked to keep tourists from wandering up the stairs at all hours.

An unmarked car was parked along the street, and Detective Bailey was standing out on the sand. The wind had picked up and was ruffling his short hair.

She left the bag in her locked car and joined him on the beach.

Detective Bailey was standing next the hole in the sand where Angie had found the briefcase a few hours earlier, making notes on his notepad. He looked up at Angie as she got close to him.

"We're assuming that he fell. What we know is that he hit, or was hit, on his forehead with blunt force trauma that would be consistent with either falling off something or being hit with something."

"Can you get more specific than that?"

"I could, but not to you."

She made a face. "So you know more about the bruise than you're saying, but you're willing to admit that it was caused by some kind of blunt force."

"That is correct."

"And..." She looked around, squinting to help keep the sand out of her eyes. "You're trying to figure out what killed him."

"Just so."

"Which is why you called me out here," she joked, "because if anyone should know about hitting someone with a blunt object, it's a bookseller. We smack around our customers all the time."

He rolled his eyes and turned away from her.

Why *had* he called her?

Was he considering her as a suspect? And he wanted to gauge her reaction to being here. Would she try to steer him away from something? It still seemed like a nice gesture. The two of them hadn't exactly hit it off the last time he'd questioned her.

She cleared her throat. "I...uh...looked through Reed's papers."

"Of course you did."

"Let me tell you what I think he was doing. Unless you're just going to arrest me now, in which case I want a lawyer."

"Walter Snuock coming back to the island for the gala, eh?"

The sting had come out of nowhere. She practically jumped. Not that she really minded being razzed a little. It was just so unexpected.

"Am I under arrest, officer?" She held her wrists in front of her.

He waved a hand, not bothering to look at her. "I'm sorry. This case. It was already touch and go with the sudden influx of tourists from this treasure hunt thing. To have to sort out a probable murder in a situation like this, where people are coming and going all the time, well, I won't lie. We're all a little tense down at the police station anyway."

"At least you're not having the screaming fits about it," she muttered.

"What was that?"

"Nothing important. Just..." She took a breath and let it out. "I'll try to stay focused, sorry. What I think Reed was looking for was information on a forged painting."

"What?"

"He didn't say to me specifically, but he mentioned something about an impostor in his email to me, and his briefcase is full of information on forgeries. He doesn't have any personal notes explaining any of it, or course, but that's what I think. He was very private."

"All right," Detective Bailey said. "He thought the Monet was forged?"

"I'm not sure about that, but I think so."

"Angie, that's a pretty flimsy lead. It's not proof, but sometimes a flimsy lead is better than a poke in the eye with a sharp stick."

She blinked. Now *there* was a colorful metaphor.

She stared across the beach toward the water. The sand was even and free of rocks and trash. The boats had been moved off the beach for the winter, and the little building had been practically nailed shut against the storms. Not a single window was in sight.

In other words, nothing that could cause blunt force trauma was in sight. Which meant that whatever had caused Reed's bruise was somewhere else.

The most obvious place to hide a weapon would be in the water. And they already knew that the killer had come near the water, both to bury the briefcase in the sand and to drag Reed's body away from shore.

"Do you know about Locard's Exchange Principle?" Detective Bailey said suddenly.

"No, what is it? Who was that?"

"The Sherlock Holmes of France. One of the pioneers of forensic science. His idea was that every contact leaves a trace. Not just murderers, but everyone, everywhere. Everything. But he focused on criminals. They leave something, they take something with them."

"You think the murderer took the murder weapon with him and didn't just drop it into the harbor? If he buried the briefcase, why wouldn't he bury the murder weapon?"

"I think that if the victim was murdered here, of all places, then he had to have come here on foot. I think he, or she for that matter, meant to come back for the briefcase," Detective Bailey said. "We've been able to establish that he didn't rent a car. And why would he have ridden with someone he didn't know?"

Angie remembered Jasper's suggestion that Reed had planned to meet with someone, maybe a lover, on the island without mentioning it to her, but Detective Bailey seemed to be on a roll, so she didn't interrupt.

"So he came here on foot," Detective Bailey said again. He was pacing back and forth on the sand now, looking at his shoes, going so far as to pull up the legs of his trousers in order to look at them.

"And got sand in his clothes? *Did* he have sand in his clothes?"

"Yes, and it's consistent with the sand that's on this part of the beach."

"And you think the killer has sand in his clothes as well."

Wait...was he trying to tell her that he had a suspect? Had he found sand on someone else's clothes?

Detective Bailey looked up at her suddenly. "There's a lot of sand on an island," he said. "And a lot of the sand on Nantucket is consistent with this beach."

She shook her head. "Whatever you're trying to get at, I'm not following you."

He straightened up, holding one hand to shade his eyes, and turned around in a slow circle. "I don't know what I think yet. I need to get back to the office. I thank you, ma'am, for meeting me out here; it's saved me a little time today, on a day where I don't have time to spare."

They walked back up to the street. She handed over the garbage bag with the briefcase, book, and papers, and he drove off, giving her a little wave as he passed.

What had *that* all been about?

~

The first thing she did when she got back to the bookstore was look up the book from Reed's briefcase and put a copy on order. She should have read it from cover to cover when she had it here in the shop instead of giving way to shock and grief. But it's easy to forget what one *should* do when one is carried away by strong emotions, as Victor Nouges's mysterious lady had proved oh-so-long ago.

The second thing she did was to start educating herself on the world of forgery. She spent a half an hour speed reading articles online, learning in the process that forgeries were typically sold on the black market first before popping up in legitimate auctions. The articles were interesting, but not detailed. What she really needed was a book on forgeries. Maybe some in depth research would give her a little more insight into Reed's so-called "quest."

The third thing she did was stand up abruptly as the door opened behind her. Jo and Mickey were there—not carrying pastries boxes this time, but simply *there*—with arms outstretched.

Angie collected hugs from both of them.

"We're getting you out of here," Jo said.

"I've been in and out all day, really," Angie said. She didn't add that she was waiting to find out whether Walter was coming back this evening or tomorrow morning.

"I've already called Aunt Margery," Jo said. "We have permission." She leaned forward so that she could see into the bookstore and waved at Aunt Margery. Aunt Margery waved back.

"Where are we going?"

"Sheldon's."

"You're going to make me fat," she said, giving in.

"Sit around and eat all day?" Mickey said. "Fat sounds awesome. Let's do fat."

~

Angie was surprised to discover that she was starving when she walked in the door of Sheldon's. Starving, and suddenly panicky. It was weird. The feelings that had been so overwhelming when she was here last—waiting for Reed and worrying about him—seemed to be waiting for her on her return.

But it was something she could master, even if it did force her to stand stock still in the doorway for a couple of breaths. . As she walked into the restaurant, Jeanette standing at the maître-d' stand, watched her with her head tilted.

"Are you well, ma chère?"

Angie said, "I just remembered the last time I was here."

"Eh, poor thing." Jeanette came around the stand and gave her a hug. "No better cure for grief than to eat. Can you eat?"

"I can eat," Angie said firmly. Her stomach growled obligingly, and Jeanette squeezed her tighter before letting her go.

"Follow me," she said, and led them through the restaurant to the kitchen.

The quiet jazz music and muted buzz of conversation transitioned into the hustle and bustle of the restaurant kitchen. Clanks, bangs, and loud rock music filled the room, as did the smell of sautéed garlic and freshly cooked seafood. In one corner of the kitchen, a small outdoor café table had been set up for the three of them. A chef's table.

A pan dropped on the floor, sounding like a gong.

Sheldon bellowed, "How many times do I have to tell you not to do that?"

"Just one more time, boss. One more time."

"Don't *do* that!"

Laughter.

Jeanette said, "You will not be ordering this evening. You will be fed. Is that understood?"

"Yes, ma'am," they all said.

Jeanette clapped twice, seeming to grow a foot taller as her face took on a stern look. "Then let the food begin!"

The feast commenced with genuine foie gras on toasted brioche. Angie was shocked. She knew that fattened goose liver wasn't easy to get in the States, and it was terrifically expensive, especially for the small amount that she and the Jerritts were eating.

Then she noticed that *everyone* was eating it. Some of the cooks at the stations were feeding it to each other as they cooked, so no one would miss out.

Then came langoustines, which were lobster-like creatures that were just as delicious as their larger cousins, with a homemade tarragon mayonnaise, lemon wedges, a variety of crudités, and thin slices of sourdough bread. Finger food.

Jeanette had disappeared back to the front of the restaurant, but Sheldon was still moving around the kitchen, looking over the cooks' shoulders, tasting a few things here and there, and cracking joking. The thing that most amused Angie was how noisy it was. From the front of the restaurant, you'd never suspect the relaxed but *loud* chaos happening a few steps away.

Mickey said, "So that guy who was at the café this afternoon?"

"Oh yes," Angie said. Her strange meeting with Detective Bailey on the beach had briefly put Mr. Motorcycle out of her mind. "Wyatt Gilmore? How was he? I was trying to pull him out of his shell. He started talking about basketball for a while, but then he clammed up again."

"Yeah, the poor guy. He's had a rough year. His brain is dripping out of his ears. But it sounds like he's pretty good at what he does. Or what he *did*. He got fired. He told you that, right?"

"I seem to remember that he did. Or he implied it at least. A data analyst, right?"

"That's it. Anyway, I hooked him up with some of my friends from college who are running some kind of, well, I don't like to say it's a scam, but it's a scam. They're running a lot of data analysis on basketball numbers and making a lot of well-informed bets."

"That does sound like a scam. Do I know these guys?"

"You mean, did you meet 'em?" He chortled to himself. "You must not have. These aren't people you can forget."

Mickey proceeded to tell them all about his college friends: three computer programmers whose official job was to hack into banks and then charge exorbitant fees to teach them how to fix their security issues. Once Angie heard the name of the company, it dropped into place—she'd heard about them back when she was working at the investment firm.

"Do you think it'll be a good fit?" she asked.

"For Wyatt? No idea," Mickey admitted. "I mean, the best you can do is put people in the same room and see if they click. But it might work. He's desperate."

Angie's eyes went wide as she was struck by an idea.

"Um, Angie? You have something you want to tell us?" said Mickey between mouthfuls of bread.

"Well, yeah, I guess." She replied, "I think Reed was looking into something about forged paintings. I learned recently that most of the forgeries start on the black market."

Mickey swallowed his mouthful of food, and shot a glance over at his sister.

"Angie, this was supposed to be a night off. No work. No Walter. No murder mysteries. No treasure hunts." Said Jo.

"Okay, okay," Angie replied, "But let me just finish this one thought and we'll move on."

Jo shrugged, and Mickey nodded in agreement.

"Mickey, could you get your friends to help me do some black market research on the world of forgery?" Asked Angie.

"Yeah, sure." Said Mickey grinning, "If it's illegal and online, these guys can help. They owe me a favor or two so I'll ask them tomorrow. Now, back to food?"

Angie sipped her wine and smiled, "Deal."

She chewed on a slice of sourdough. Out of the corner of her eye, she caught Jo staring into space while sitting on her hands.

"Jo...are you all right?"

"Sure."

"You haven't said a word all night."

Jo wasn't normally the quiet type.

"Sorry. Too many things on my mind."

"Like what?"

She made a face. "Business stuff. They don't tell you, when you're a young punk with razorblades dangling off the safety pins on your leather jacket, if you don't want to work for the man then someday you'll have to learn how to run a business ."

"You totally work for the man," Mickey said. She hit him in the arm, her face relaxing into a smile.

"I don't work for you."

"Do so."

In a minute they were having the world's most ridiculous slappy-fight, right at the chef's table. Sheldon cleared his throat from across the room. "All right, children, settle down. Someone will bring you oysters in a minute...but only if you're good."

They laughed and settled back in their chairs. Mickey grabbed the last piece of sourdough and munched on it.

"Go on," Angie said.

"Honestly, though? I kind of like running a business," Jo said.

This had been obvious to Angie for years now, but she nodded as though the information had been some kind of big revelation.

"I like doing almost the same thing every day. I like running the numbers. I like paying the bills. The boring stuff. I like it."

"Is that really what's on your mind?"

"Honestly? I'm mentally counting up the bank account and realizing that we have extra money to play with, and I'm wondering what to do with it, and afraid of screwing it up. Advertising? Repairs?"

"Buy a new oven?" Mickey suggested helpfully. "We could buy a new oven."

"It's not that much money."

They bickered for a few moments longer. Then one of the cooks brought over a plate of oysters Rockefeller and another plate of fresh Blue Points. A second later he was back, with all the trimmings and a basket of hush puppies.

"Good, good," Sheldon called from the other side of the kitchen.

Jo sank back into her reverie, occasionally pulling a notebook out of her jacket to jot something down.

Mickey said, "Do you ever think about us?"

It came out of the blue. Angie actually had to blink at him for several seconds before she even realized what he was talking about. In high school, the two of them had dated for a while, but it hadn't worked out. It felt so long ago. Ancient history.

"Not often," she admitted. "Mostly I'm wrapped up in things closer to the present."

"Now that you're dating Walter, I think about it more," he admitted.

Well, that was awkward. What was she supposed to say to that?

"Oh?" was what she finally settled on. She didn't know what she expected him to say next. It was Mickey; he might go off on a tangent about how the situation reminded him of his favorite type of pastry flour. He might turn it into a joke.

But he didn't.

"I should have said something when you came back. Before it was too late."

Angie blinked again. She had been back for almost three years now. He'd had plenty of time if he'd wanted to try dating again.

He picked up one of the Blue Points, sprinkled some hot sauce on it, and gulped it down. "I don't know why I didn't. The bakery, probably. Like, we had to get it up and running before I was willing to, I don't know. Live. Do real stuff that wasn't numbers and ledger entries and trying to scrape by without having to ask anyone for help. I thought that's what you were doing, too. I thought, 'Don't bother Angie, stupid. We both have too much on our minds.'"

He shook his head. "And now? Now you've got Walter. And I realize that it was dumb to wait. Life doesn't do that. One second someone's there. The next they're gone."

Angie said, "Mickey..."

"Don't stress it, though," he said. "I mean, look at you and Walter. He's a good guy. You obviously click. And it would suck if things had gone awkward again. What if we'd dated for serious and then we weren't happy with each other? That gets awkward fast, even more awkward than me talking to you about this stuff now. I mean, one minute you're making out, and the next minute the circus comes to town and I run off with the bearded lady. Heartbreak city. What *would* you do without me?"

Angie cracked up. She couldn't help it.

When she got her breath back, she opened her mouth to say something tactful.

Mickey raised a hand palm-out. "You don't have to say anything. I know, you're really upset that you took me for granted for so long, but let's face it. I was always going to leave you for a sasquatch or something. Let's just leave it at that and move on with our lives."

So she closed her mouth again and ate another oyster.

"That's *my* oyster," he said.

She took another one and downed it, shoving his hands away as he jokingly tried to steal it.

∼

After a main course of sirloin with béarnaise sauce and Jeanette's mashed potatoes—which were loaded with enough butter, garlic, and cream to give a healthy person a heart attack—they struggled to finish with a chocolate stout mousse served with raspberries and whipped cream, and finally failed.

Sheldon didn't seem to mind; he stood over their little chef's table and gloated, literally rubbing his hands together as he cackled, saying things like, "I have defeated the Jerritt twins this day. Bow before me," and other complete nonsense that made them all laugh.

On their way out, they spotted the Beauchamps at a table. Mr. Beauchamp waved them over and gave them a loud and conspiratorial whisper: "We've made progress!"

"On what?" Angie asked.

"On the mystery!"

"Oh, hush, Charles," whispered Mrs. Beauchamp. "You're overstating things *just* a little."

Her voice sounded playful, but her eyes looked nervously around the room. They fastened on the same person that caught Angie's eyes: Alayna Karner. Alayna was by herself at a small table, fixedly staring at the five of them.

"We think..." Mr. Beauchamp leaned in even closer. "...that we've found the location of the painting!"

"Oh, Charles!" Mrs. Beauchamp said in a low voice. "Don't pull their legs like that!"

"It's in—" Suddenly Mr. Beauchamp jumped, and twisted around in his chair. "Darling! Why did you kick me?"

"*She...is...watching!*" Mrs. Beauchamp said, jerking her head toward Alayna Karner.

Mr. Beauchamp turned in the direction Mrs. Beauchamp was looking. His eyes widened and his posture straightened until he was puffing out his skinny chest. Then his eyes narrowed.

"I shall tell you at a later time," he said.

"If you think you know where the painting is, you should tell them at the Chamber of Commerce first," Angie said. "That way, your guess will be registered."

Mrs. Beauchamp put her hand to her face, as if to say, *Here we go again.*

"I refuse to tell the Chamber of Commerce," Mr. Beauchamp said. "*Someone is sabotaging that office.* Mark my words. That office has had more trouble than a barrel full of monkeys ever since we got here. Computers going down, bad service, information lost!"

"What information was lost?" Angie said, who could understand Mr. Beauchamp's first two of his complaints, but was puzzled by the last one.

"Pamphlets! Books! Maps! Every so-called 'lead' they give us leads nowhere, or else it's missing!" Mr. Beauchamp looked at his wife. "Isn't that right, Dottie?"

"Yes, Charles," she said.

"Couldn't that be due to, forgive me, some unethical treasure hunters?" Angie asked.

"You betcha," Mr. Beauchamp said. "But *who*?"

"What does that have to do with the Chamber of Commerce?"

"*There's a traitor in the office, can't you see?*" Mr. Beauchamp hissed. "Someone has to be one step ahead of us. One. Step. Ahead. Either it's a traitor in the office or it's a hacker, breaking into their computer, stealing information, and feeding it back to their treasure hunter on the island!"

Mr. Beauchamp settled back in his chair, smug.

"But we've gotten around all that, haven't we, Dottie? And if they get too close"—he glared at Alayna Karner—"then we have our own defenses. They'll regret getting in our way, won't they, Dot?"

Mrs. Beauchamp seemed to sink into herself. "Oh, Charles. It's not that important."

"Not important?" His voice carried. "Winning is not important?"

A slim hand dropped onto Mr. Beauchamp's shoulder. Jeanette. "Is everything all right?"

Mr. Beauchamp glared at her. "Your fine establishment never

disappoints, Madame. But that…that *spy* has followed us here. She refuses to leave us alone. She can't find the painting herself, so she follows in our footsteps, hoping to steal all the glory from us like some sort of vulture!"

He raised one shaking finger to point at Alayna Karner.

Jeanette took in the situation with a carefully blank face. "Would you like me to move your table elsewhere? We have a private chef's table inside the kitchen that has only just been vacated, if you don't mind the noise."

"In the kitchen?" Mr. Beauchamp exclaimed. "Why, don't mind if we do."

And, without a backward glance, Jeanette led them out of the room. A moment later, a server appeared to take their glasses and plates.

Alayna Karner watched them leave. Then her eyes fixed on Angie.

"Let's get out of here," Jo said. "That woman has a face in need of a good smack."

"Backpfeifengesicht," Mickey said.

"Gesundheit," Angie said.

"It's German," Mickey said, as Jo led them out of the restaurant, "for 'a face for slapping.'"

Angie remembered Mr. Beauchamp's earlier implications that Mrs. Beauchamp had poisoned someone as a nurse. She just hoped that nobody decided Alayna's face was in need of something worse than a slap. Tensions were rising.

As bad as the situation was, she realized, it could still get worse.

Chapter 11

TURN DOWN THE VOLUME

Her phone had two messages on it, one from Walter and the other from Detective Bailey. The volume, she noticed, had been turned off. Angie held out the phone and jiggled it in front of Jo. "Did you, or did anyone you know, steal my phone when I wasn't looking and turn off the volume?"

Jo smirked. "I'm not saying I did. But I'm not saying I didn't."

"I'm not saying you're a bad person. But I'm not saying you're *not* a bad person. I had messages from both Walter *and* Detective Bailey."

"What? Are they more important than we are?" Jo put a hand to her forehead and pretended to swoon.

"You're impossible," Angie said. But she noticed that Mickey's face had fallen. She decided that, when everything settled down again, she'd have to do something to make sure their friendship wouldn't suffer. Mickey had joshed her into feeling better about his confession, but he was obviously still feeling bad about it himself.

Later.

They dropped her off in the parking lot behind the bookstore. She called Detective Bailey first while walking up to the bookstore, which was still open.

"Ms. Prouty," he said, "I need you to come pick up the book that was in Reed's briefcase, read it for me, and report back to me on whether you find any clues."

She stopped in mid-stride, putting her foot down heavily and almost stumbling.

"You want me to read a *book* for you?"

"My eyes are swimming and I can't make heads or tails of it. Besides, I you are the only person on the island who is a certified speed reader. I trust you can read through these love letters better than I can."

"You can't make heads or tails of a bunch of love letters?"

He sounded relieved. "That's right. They're impossible. Written in all this flowery language and I can't be sure what anybody means because nobody comes right out and says anything. It's going right over my head."

"And—" She'd been about to say, *And nobody else at the police station can read?* But that wasn't fair at all—just snarky. Besides, she actually really *did* want to read the book herself.

"I apologize, but I have to wrap things up at the bookstore," she said, switching gears. "Is there any way you could drop the book off here? Or I could pick it up at the station, but it'll be late."

"I'll drop it off," Detective Bailey said. "You just stay put until I get there."

"Shouldn't be a problem," she said, and stepped inside the back door of the bookstore. She hung up her coat, dropped her phone in her pocket, and turned toward the front of the house.

Walter was standing next to Aunt Margery, looking over her shoulder at something on the computer screen.

Angie smiled. "Walter!"

He straightened up and turned toward her, mirroring her smile. As their eyes met, a sense of quiet contentment washed over Angie. It was as if the very sight of him had restored gravity to a world in which she had felt herself free-floating from one disaster to the next. It was too early to decided whether she truly loved him, but the affection and attraction she felt toward him were undeniable.

Walter swept her up in a tight hug. "I'm so sorry about Reed," he said. "I know the two of you were close."

She settled into the hug with conflicting emotions. One the one hand, she felt safe and calm for the first time since this whole treasure hunt business started, but on the other, the thought of Reed still made her heart ache. She drew in a deep breath and conquered her urge to cry. There was really no point in getting Walter's shirt wet.

She finally stepped back. "I...thank you. But we weren't really close. Reed was so private."

She felt like she'd been saying that all day, almost like an apology.

Walter said firmly, "The two of you *were* close. You mentioned him several times to me. Just because you didn't know much about him didn't mean that you weren't a friend of his. You were his friend. You were close."

His words were strangely validating. It felt almost as if Walter had just given her permission to grieve. "Thank you. You're right. He was important to me, even if I didn't know all the details of his life."

He hugged her again. "How are you holding up?"

"I've been better," she said into his chest.

He stroked her back in sympathy.

After a moment, she pulled away again and did a quick sweep of the bookstore. There weren't many customers, but those that were present seemed settled and content. It was peaceful enough that Captain Parfait had come out of hiding and had climbed up into his accustomed spot by the front window. The first few nights that Angie had stayed open late, he had pouted over the change in his schedule. But even he seemed to be adapting.

She checked on Janet, who was jiggling from one foot to the other in boredom. She had long since cleaned and restocked the café area. Angie suggested that she relocate to the computer in the stock room to identify the software she would need to start designing ad materials for the store, and she broke out in a wide smile.

"You're serious about this?"

"Of course," Angie said.

"What's my budget?"

"None, yet. I want you to pick your dream software, and then your 'okay, I can make this work' backup software and email me with the prices and links and the logic behind your choices."

"Okay!"

Off she went.

Aunt Margery was working on ordering stock for the week—a task that Angie normally handled. Angie reminded herself that she was making a serious effort not to micromanage, especially when she knew her staff was qualified to do the work. Aunt Margery had a good sense for what readers liked and didn't like that stretched far beyond her love of Ruth Rendell. It would be fine.

She turned back to Walter. "Is everything ready for the Gala?"

"It seems to be," he said. "Unfortunately, I have no idea whether it really is or not. Everyone smiles at me and tells me that everything is going smoothly and that this whole treasure hunter thing is the best thing that happened on the island, and so on, and I have no idea what's really going on. I get the impression that there's molten chaos bubbling just under the surface, about to erupt."

She laughed.

"I've never organized anything big before," he admitted. "It's a lot more work than I anticipated. I thought I could handle most of this by myself, in between cases at work. Boy, was I wrong."

She laughed again. "I remember my first festival on the island. I was a mess. Aunt Margery was ready to kill me…I swear, the Jerritt twins spent more time helping me than they did in their own booth."

"But you seemed so organized when I saw you last July," he said.

She shook her head. "When that first festival was over, I wrote out a plan so that I would never be that unprepared again. I screw up all the time. I just try not to make the same mistakes twice."

"An admirable philosophy," he said. "I don't know if I can manage it, personally. I seem to be making the same mistakes over and over."

"Oh?" she said.

Just then, the back door opened, and Detective Bailey walked in, looking exhausted.

"Coffee?" she called to him.

"Yes, please."

She checked the coffee pots, but they'd all been cleaned. An Americano it was. She started making it.

Behind her, she heard the two men talking.

"Hello, Mr. Snuock."

"Hello, Detective Bailey. Are you working on Mr. Edgerton's death?"

Detective Bailey paused for a moment, then said, "That I am."

"Any new developments you can share?"

"A few. But I'm just about beat…ask Ms. Prouty about 'em, if you'd like to know."

The conversation sounded very stiff, but without sarcasm or rancor.

"Angie knows everything, doesn't she?" Aunt Margery said.

"She sure does, ma'am," Detective Bailey said. "In fact I've come to—"

If Angie put off pulling the shot too much longer, it would be obvious that she was listening in. She started the espresso machine. The noise wiped out the rest of the conversation. She finished the Americano, put it in a double cup, and looked over at the detective.

"Cream? Sugar?"

"Cream, and a lot of it," Detective Bailey said. "I've had a lot of bad coffee in my time, and my stomach gets sensitive these days."

She added a generous amount of cream, put the lid on, and handed it over.

The detective accepted the cup, then handed her the book that she'd taken out of Reed's briefcase. It was in a plastic bag and had obviously been fingerprinted—there were dark smudges on the clothbound cover.

"It's been tested," he said, "but I'd appreciate it if you read it with gloves on, just in case."

"I'm sure I've already left fingerprints on this," she admitted, somewhat sheepishly. She had forgotten to put her gloves back on when she took that second look inside Reed's briefcase.

"Sure. Just don't add any others, if you can help it. I'm already catching crap for letting you read it in the first place. The only way I got permission was to threaten to leave the book with the chief and make *her* read it instead. Suddenly, I had all the permission I needed."

Angie smiled. She just couldn't see what was so difficult about a book full of love letters. But then again she was a reader, from a family of readers, working as a professional reader selling books for a living. The tables would probably be turned if suddenly she needed someone to pull a license plate number for her.

"How soon do you need to know if there's anything in the book?" she asked.

"The sooner the better, honestly. We don't have much to go on."

Angie nodded, wondering what he was holding back. "Thank you. I'll get on this right away."

"Thank you, Ms. Prouty. And now I'll be off." He nodded to all of them, then left via the back door, sipping his coffee.

Walter said, "He always gives me the impression that he has no idea what he's doing, is barely listening, and couldn't care less. But he dealt with Dad's murder pretty well…I think it's an act."

Angie said, "I'm starting to think so, too. I have to admit he didn't make the best impression on me when I first met him, either."

That night, Angie read the little book of love letters. She kept a notebook and jotted down her impressions as she went.

It *wasn't* easy reading, as a matter of fact, or at least not when she tried to read it through Detective Bailey's eyes. Aside from the dated language and the fact that each letter was written for one reader in particular, there was a confusing lack of context. Were the couple married? Where did they come from? Who were the other people they referenced? The editor had written an introduction to each letter pointing out juicy bits, particularly well-written lines, and other trivia, but it was rare that those introductions provided any details about the letter writers.

Angie was almost at the end when a particular passage leapt out at her.

Ma chère, my beloved, my stranger from another land, I feel as though I have always wanted you, and, having lost you, I will always want you. For the rest of my life, I shall be in longing for you. Do not think that it is a longing that drives me to despair. It seems to color my every waking moment with heartbreak, and yet it is a sensation that I will never, ever relinquish. I adore you, and in not having you, my adoration transforms this entire island into a paradise, the place where I once held you, and loved you, and now is colored forever with the memories I have made with you here. It seems as though the entire island has become a painting, a shimmering wash of color. I look at the water, the boats on the water, and I think of the painting that you have given to me. My world has become that painting. I live in it, in between the dabs of color that shimmer in the summer light.

It sounded beautiful, although Angie had to wonder how long that particular flavor of romance had lasted. She remembered when she had first fallen in love with Doug, and how wonderful everything had seemed at first. Everything had tugged on Angie's heartstrings back then. Clouds dappled with sunlight? Romantic. A little kid in a stroller with its parents? Romantic. Small dogs, cappuccino cups, rain, leaves in the wind, the chime of silver on china...everything.

Maybe these lovers had fallen hard for each other and split apart just before things could go wrong.

She shook her head. Too cynical. She had to stop comparing everyone else's love life to hers and Doug's. He was a terrible measuring stick.

She read the passage again, then closed the book and riffled through the pages. As expected, the book fell open to the same page.

It was an older book, published in—she flipped to the front—1963. It was over four hundred pages long. The end of the book gave a few sources, mostly for the most famous love letters (James Joyce had penned one of them, for instance). The editor had written a long-running column in a Los Angeles newspaper in which she had published anonymous and famous love letters. Back in the day, you could send a copy of a love letter to the newspaper, and they'd publish it with the identifying details removed. In the book, the details had been replaced by italicized text and footnotes stating things like, "This name has been changed to protect the identities of the lovers."

She read the letter again.

It started out with a few paragraphs of local news. References to Nantucket and its old railroad caught her eye, but they were written in such vague terms that she wasn't surprised she had missed them the first time. For instance, one section read: *I can only hope that your business has been successfully concluded. I know how much your father depends on you, and of course your contributions to the struggle at hand shall be vital for the success of all of us.* The "business concluded" clearly reference the railroad purchase, and the "struggle at hand" must allude to the First World War. The writer's meaning wasn't hard to discern when one knew some background information, but without that knowledge, it was nearly impenetrable.

The subject matter of the letter shifted from news to romance after a few paragraphs. The author wrote of her love for her correspondent and of her certainty of his love for her. She missed him and regretted that she would have to continue with her life as if nothing had happened. Although she wanted to stay in touch with him, it was probably for the best if she didn't—she could think of no valid excuse to keep up a correspondence with a male acquaintance in another country. The tone of the letter turned wistful. Perhaps at Christmas he could send her a note? But maybe it would be best if he didn't.

The end of the letter was increasingly forlorn. The undercurrent of longing throughout the letter now seemed more like pleading. The writer managed to keep herself from openly begging her lover to return, but only just.

The postscript was brief, saying only that she had moved the painting to a place where it would be hidden and safe from damage, and where she could see it once a year on the anniversary of their parting. In a firm tone, she told her lover to ignore what she had said before and never to contact her again, saying that the lover had relinquished all rights to her when he had left.

She was letting go of him, almost pushing him away.

It was a sad letter—a prolonged goodbye that began in warmth yet ended coldly. The break in tone between the body of the letter and the postscript was striking, almost as if something had happened in between them—an event that the lady did not directly refer to at all.

Had she been found out by her fiancé? By a family member? Was the painting found? Did something happen to it? How did this relate to Reed's search for an art forger?

She typed up an email for Detective Bailey summing up the book, identifying the letter and in fact typing the whole thing out for him to look at. It wasn't much, she had to admit, in the way of additional clues.

Then she read the rest of the book. Nothing else popped out.

The next morning, Angie opened the store, served her gentlemen their coffee and newspapers and let them chatter themselves out, then closed up again so she could go to the library. She left behind a note that said, "Minor emergency—will return by ten thirty."

The library was nearly dead. She was greeted by the longsuffering librarian, who had ample experience with Angie's research kicks. There had been a time when Angie would come to the library, order a dozen books on a particular subject, and spend all day doing searches through databases for information. But that had been a while ago. Angie had since subscribed to several databases on her own, and she now did more of her book research from the store during off hours.

Today's research subject was art forgery. Mickey's friends were going to get her some information from the dark corners of the modern internet, but Angie was looking for historical information. First, she searched for old news articles about sales of paintings and started making a list of major transactions starting at 1900. Next, she started searches for known sales of forged paintings that had been caught, but quickly hit a dead end. There was plenty of records about legitimate painting sales, but precious little about forgeries. She had to hope Mickey's friends could cross reference her list of actual transactions and try to figure out when potential forgeries had changed hands.

She put everything away and started dragging her feet back to the bookstore. On the way through the library, however, she noticed a black motorcycle jacket hanging on the back of one of the chairs in front of the library computers, the ones that could be checked out by patrons.

Wyatt Gilmore was here. She knew it. As a data analyst, no doubt he'd spent time combing through the records held in the library. She sniffed. It wasn't like he had anything better to do; of course he had a head start. Then she chided herself. *She* was more interested in finding out if the Monet was a forgery, and who might have murdered Reed. It didn't matter to her if Wyatt found the painting.

What she should do was take Wyatt into her confidence, give him the information that she'd discovered, and let him run with it. Finding the painting would be a feather in his cap, both financially, and as proof that he was good at his job. She wouldn't be able to claim the prize money regardless.

But first she should get permission from Detective Bailey. She hurried out the door before Wyatt could spot her and ask her what she was doing. She was already late, anyway.

∼

The rest of the day passed in a blur. Janet had the day off, and Aunt Margery had called to say that she wanted to take some time off to finish a book that had just come out. She wanted to skip the gala anyway. Angie laughed and told her to skive off with a clear conscience.

The store was busy, but pleasantly so, and of course they were closing early for the gala. Everyone in town was.

Originally, Walter had wanted to have the gala at his father's old house on the hill, but that was on the opposite side of the island. Carol Brightwell over at the Chamber of Commerce had talked him into having it at the Whaling Museum instead, and opening it up to the tourists in town. His agreement had been reluctant at first, but when Angie checked in with him at two, he sounded relieved.

"I can't imagine what I would have done if I had tried to have the gala at home," he said at least three times. "I always assumed that Dad kept the house closed up from the public because he was a miser and didn't want to deal with people, but now I'm starting to wonder. I've just had to listen to an extended lecture about parking. And the number and availability of toilets. And facilities for the handicapped. It's all important, and it's all stuff that never crossed my mind. You'd think it would have, because, hey, lawyer, but no. I feel like I'm being dragged through a crash course in hospitality."

She said a few soothing things about how it was all overwhelming at first, but would soon settle into a routine. "There's no shame in having someone like Carol on your side, giving you advice," she said. "In a way, this is all new to you."

"What, being rich or being generous?" he said drily. "Never mind. I'm just complaining. As one of my old law school professors used to say, 'You trade up for those problems.'"

She laughed. "It gets easier, I promise."

"I sure hope you're right. And I *am* going to hold a gala or something at the house next year, even if it means I have to rip out the front steps and build a parking lot. I'm determined."

"Next Christmas," she said.

He sighed.

"What time are you coming over?" he asked wistfully.

"I'm closing at three, so probably by five."

"Five?"

"I have about an hour of things to do after closing, and then I'll go home and shower and eat something."

"There's going to be food here."

"There's going to be a little food and a *lot* of alcohol," she said. "I'm such a lightweight…I have to eat before I got out for things like this, or I'll spend the whole night being cranky."

"All right," he said reluctantly.

"I highly advise getting something to eat before you get your tux on," Angie said.

"There's too much to do."

"If you honestly think that you really have anything to do other than show up, then you don't know the crews at the Chamber of Commerce and the Whaling Museum," Angie said. "I know it's been chaotic, but they really do know what they're doing. They do this every year for the Festival of Lights, so they're a well-oiled machine by now. You'll be fine. Grab a sandwich."

Right before she closed up for the day, Mickey came over with another box of pastries, which she didn't need. A few people lingered in the bookstore, but most of them had already left.

"Food?" he asked.

"I need real food," she said. "Not cupcakes."

"I forgot the gala was tonight. Nobody wants the late delivery."

"Take them over to the museum. They'll get eaten, at least."

"True." He put the boxes down and leaned against the edge of the counter. "Jo's not coming tonight."

"What?"

"Her boyfriend's mom is having health problems on the mainland...a heart attack? It sounded bad. Anyway, she took off on the ferry."

Angie checked her phone and found she had a message from Jo that she'd missed earlier. The volume had been "helpfully" turned down again. Fortunately, she hadn't missed anything else of importance.

"That's too bad," she said.

"It is. You know what her boyfriend's like," Mickey said.

"I haven't spent a lot of time with him," Angie admitted. "Jo's been really private about dating him."

It was true, she realized. Jo going through the first flush of falling in love had been alternately effusive and absent a lot.

"Well, you know he's a punk."

Angie smiled. She'd never admit it, but seeing Jo and her similarly mohawked boyfriend holding hands and smiling at each other was decidedly adorable.

"Yes, but you can hear him sobbing in the background of Jo's voicemail. He's a piece of mush."

"You probably should be a piece of mush if your mom's in the hospital."

"True."

Mickey pulled away from the counter, gave her a sloppy salute, and picked up the pastry boxes. Angie held the door for him.

After he left, she couldn't help dwelling on the fact that Mickey still had a thing for her. For more than a few minutes she was lost in memories. But then she shook it off. She had an evening with Walter to look forward to.

Chapter 12

THE GALA

The Whaling Museum was run by the Nantucket Historical Association, a collection of curators and archivists who maintained everything from buildings to ships' logs, and who ran docent-led walking tours from May to the end of October. They were the powerhouse behind every historical effort on the island.

Walter hadn't exactly ignored them, but he hadn't made as many connections there as he had at the Chamber of Commerce. As a result, the NHA had been letting Walter run his own show, and make his own mistakes. But now that they were directly involved at the Whaling Museum, they were on point and shining.

Walter, dressed in his tux, was clearly impressed. Compared to the Chamber of Commerce, the NHA was precise, professional, and unshakable. They played politics better than the Chamber, because they had more budget at stake.

"If I ever do something like this again," Walter whispered in her ear,

"I'm going to work with these guys. They've really been educating me."

"I've always been impressed with them," Angie said. "But they're pretty regimented about what they will and will not do."

"They're pretty regimented in general."

"That's true. But I'm pretty sure they won't work with you on next year's gala unless you add a serious historical aspect to the party."

He groaned. "Next year's gala. What was I thinking?"

"You were thinking, 'I should hire an assistant.' The woman I hired has been a godsend…at least, once I stopped trying to control every single thing and let her do what she's good at."

He grinned at her. "Difficult?"

"Very."

There was a champagne glass in her hand, which always made her feel a bit decadent. Her sleeveless black silk dress was covered with sequins in a lattice pattern, and she felt fabulous. She had decided to dress like it was a Manhattan high-profile socialite party: rhinestone earrings and sparkly silver shoes and all. She was loving it. Somehow she didn't feel ridiculous dressing up for an event on the island, especially when standing next to Walter in his tux.

And wasn't he a sight tonight. Tall, dark, and handsome, with a dignity that probably came from standing in front of judges as a trial lawyer. The photographer from the newspaper had taken to snapping a picture of Walter by himself, or with Angie at his side, whenever he couldn't find something else to take a picture of. GQ was going to come calling soon.

Aunt Margery had said that she might stop in later, but Angie was almost positive that was a polite fiction. Angie had stopped to check on her at the house, and found her in bed with a stack of novels that had arrived earlier in the day at the bookstore. Angie had treated her like she was sick and fussed over her until she had been chased out of the house.

Jo had gone to the mainland, and Angie had wondered whether Mickey would show up. He did, wearing a red-and-white tuxedo with a Santa hat and a twirl-worthy white mustache and goatee, a là Colonel Sanders. It was ridiculous, and the kids all loved it. He had brought all the leftover pastries from the bakery, but they had disappeared even before the start of the party. The NHA had a collective sweet tooth.

Angie moved through the room, sometimes standing next to Walter, sometimes on her own, greeting everyone she knew and getting introduced to practically everyone she didn't. Quite a few people had come over from New York and Boston for the gala, and most of them were in formal wear. More than once, an investor approached Walter to talk about some project or other that could be built on the island by investors. Walter always replied that he'd toyed with similar plans, but he wouldn't take such a step without the agreement of everyone on the island. Careful planning would be necessary, since it would require quite the balancing act to maintain profitability while preserving the island's native charm.

"A resort on the beach to the south would have several issues," he said. "First, although it would establish a large, new business that would provide a lot of jobs for the island, they would, for the most part, be low-paying jobs. Those workers would need to be housed somewhere, and that would require low-cost housing, which is already in short supply. And it would change the whole feel of the island. We're known for being small, independent, and very quirky.

We don't need corporate culture here—we already have enough of that on the mainland. We have to make sure that we're not killing the goose that lays the golden eggs."

And so on.

Angie was impressed by how fast Walter was on his feet. It was the lawyer coming out again.

She was whisked off to join a group of Aunt Margery's friends. She sipped at her champagne, nibbled on the hors d'oeuvres, and laughed at other people's jokes. She wasn't normally the kind of person who thrived on being in the middle of a crowd, but tonight it felt like nothing could wear her out.

Then she noticed Alayna Karner in the crowd. She was dressed in a sparkling red sleeveless top and black slacks. Her long, dark hair hung perfectly straight. She wore toeless black ankle boots, a chunky gold bracelet, and gold earrings. She seemed to have shed all her awkwardness and was chatting pleasantly with several people—one of whom Angie had been introduced to previously as one of Walter's friends, a Manhattan lawyer. She was nodding and smiling, managing not to look as though she were brown-nosing at all.

Alayna was looking around the room as Walter's friend introduced her to the other members of his group. She began chatting with them again. But then, her eyes fastened on Walter, who was on the other side of the room. She spoke briefly to the group around her, then turned and left them, heading toward Walter.

Stay away from him!

Angie surprised by her own reaction. It was logical that if Alayna Karner knew one of Walter's friends, she might know him as well. But Angie didn't feel jealous. She'd had plenty of experience with that poisonous emotion around Doug, so she wasn't a stranger to the feeling. Instead, she felt alert and tense, like something terrible was about to happen. There was something wrong about Alayna's body language, and Angie didn't like it.

She excused herself, handed her full champagne glass to the first passing server, and moved toward Walter as quickly as the packed room would allow.

Walter was talking to a pair of women in dark, silky opera gowns. Both were at least eighty years old and somehow were making Walter blush.

He glanced away from them for an instant and spotted Alayna Karner. His eyes widened slightly, and he took a step backward.

Angie cut straight through the middle of a group of young men, but trying to hurry through the gala crowd was proving difficult. At least she was wearing high heels, so she could see what was going on. Someone called her name, but she ignored them as she tried to sidle past the young men surrounding her.

By the time she reached the other side, Alayna was in Walter's face, shaking a finger at him. The two older ladies had left, so now Walter was on his own, pressed up against a wall. Alayna was angry about something, but she was also smiling, showing far too many teeth.

Angie danced around another crowd of people, trying not to step on any toes. A hand grabbed her arm. She looked up to see a red suit. Mickey.

"I'll distract her. You save our illustrious host," he said, then plowed forward.

People who hadn't even noticed her got out of the way immediately when a six-and-a-half-foot-tall man in a Santa tuxedo strode through the crowd. Especially once he started bellowing, "Ho ho ho! Merry Christmas," past his goatee.

He reached Alayna and Walter. "Mrs. Claus!" he exclaimed. "Finally, I have found you. Just in time for a dance."

She turned toward him and smiled automatically, a grimace melting off her lips.

Obligingly, the band, which had gone on break, started up again, playing "I Saw Mommy Kissing Santa Claus." Mickey swept the woman away from Walter and they danced through the crowd toward the open space that served as a dance floor.

"Thank you," Angie mouthed toward Mickey's back, and then she turned toward Walter.

He looked shaken. She put her arm over his and said, "Let's step out for some air."

She led him out the back door, past the serving staff. One of the back rooms had been turned into a staging area, packed with bodies and silver trays full of canapes.

Outside the air was *cold*, and Angie immediately began to shiver. It was still worth it to see Walter lean against the wall and exhale in relief.

"Thank you."

"You're welcome. Are you okay?"

"I'm fine. I just needed to get away from that woman."

Angie nodded. "She's one of the treasure hunters."

"No kidding," Walter said. "What a horrible coincidence. On second thought, that couldn't have been a coincidence at all.

Her name is Alayna Karner. Have I ever talked to you about her?"

"No."

"She was recently one of our clients at the law firm. Up for—get this—murder."

"Murder?"

"We negotiated it down to manslaughter—even though, in my not-to-be-repeated opinion, she was guilty of more than that—but she wouldn't stand for it. It went to trial. We didn't bend over backward to get her off the hook, but the D.A. made several bad mistakes, and the jury let her off on a technicality. It was ugly."

"Why is she here?" Angie asked.

"She keeps trying to harass me into dating her," he said. "I think she forgot that I'm pretty sure she murdered an ex-boyfriend."

"Brr," Angie said. "And Mickey just ran off with her. I hope he doesn't get in trouble."

"I hope so, too," Walter said. "She's crazy. I mean, just now she said something…it sounded like she was implying that she had only joined the treasure hunt so she could stalk me."

"You don't think she could have killed Reed, do you?" Angie asked.

Walter took a breath. "Good grief. I hope not. But I suppose I should talk to Detective Bailey about it anyway. I'll do it first thing tomorrow…" He pulled a phone out of his pocket and tapped away at it for a moment, leaving himself a note.

Then he glanced up. "Did you think she was an old girlfriend or something?"

"No," Angie admitted. "She's come into the bookstore and acted like a loon several times already. I managed to keep her from ripping my bookshelves down, but it was close. When I saw her moving toward you, it was more like she was a shark swimming up to her victim than an ex who wanted to rekindle an old flame."

"She's definitely a shark," Walter agreed. He took a deep breath.

"Are you going to be able to go back in there?" Angie asked.

"I'll be fine."

"Stalkers are serious," Angie said.

He made a face at her. "Believe me, I know. Trial lawyer, remember? And, even better, I'll give you three guesses as to the murder that Alayna Karner either did or didn't commit."

"Related to stalking?"

"A guy she'd had a one-night stand with. When he refused to talk to her, she ran him down with her car."

Angie shook her head. Incredible.

Suddenly, Walter surprised her by wrapping his arms around her and kissing her passionately. She felt her eyes close, one at a time, as she put her arms around his neck to steady herself. High heels could get risky.

"Thank you," Walter said again. "You're amazing, you know that?"

"You're welcome," she announced. "Although I'm going to be keeping a somewhat paranoid eye on you for the rest of the night, you know that, right? I just don't want you to think that I'm fuming with jealousy or anything."

"I won't think that," he promised, and opened the back door.

"Do you need any more time?"

"I'll be fine," he said. "Are you sure you want to be seen with me? If she sees us together, she might start following you around, too."

"She already knows where I work," Angie said. "And I'm sure that she saw us leaving together. Mickey can be distracting, but he's not *that* distracting."

"Were..." He paused. "Were the two of you together? You and Mickey?"

"Back in high school," she said. "But not since then. He's too much like a brother to me."

"Oh," Walter said, his shoulders relaxing. "Then let's go back in and face the music, shall we?"

"Does that mean I get a dance?"

"Of course."

～

The highlight of the evening was supposed to be the announcement of the winners of a silent auction that had been running all evening. The bids had been unsealed and the results viewed with some satisfaction by the NHA. Angie's main concern had been making sure that Walter hadn't auctioned himself off as a volunteer for anything. She had gone to the chairperson of the NHA, Beatrice Solly, and mentioned her concerns. The woman's eyes had widened, and she'd gone into another room to view the results again.

"Walter hasn't volunteered himself for anything like that," she confirmed, "and Miss Karner doesn't have any of the winning bids regardless."

Angie thanked her and returned to the party. Walter was currently under guard by Mickey. The two of them had been talking with their heads close together, and now they both looked at her.

Walter wore a nervous smile that quickly became more confident. Mickey had a concerned expression.

She walked up to the two of them. "Gossiping about me, I see."

Walter said, "Maybe."

Mickey said, "You okay?"

"I wish..." She turned around but didn't spot Alayna Karner anywhere. "I wish that woman hadn't come here tonight. I wish she hadn't come to the island at all. I feel tense all of a sudden, and I barely said boo to her. What about you? Did Walter give you the head's up that she might try to stalk you?"

"He did," Mickey said. "No worries. By the time we were done dancing, I had stepped on her feet about a dozen times, and I was a complete asshole to her. If she comes after me, it's going to be to improve the gene pool. I didn't make the world's best impression."

Angie chuckled.

"What about you? She was watching the two of you like a hawk. Once you got outside, she tried to get away from me and follow you."

"I'm going to take it seriously," Angie said "I'll make sure that someone always walks me out to the car, and that I'm never alone in public, and that my phone is always charged. Maybe I'll even carry mace."

"Okay. If you need any help, let me know." Mickey gave her one of his informal salutes. "Have fun, you crazy kids." He strode back into the party, reaching over a woman's head to snag a handful of canapes from a tray.

Walter took Angie's hand and squeezed it. "I think I'll be happiest if we go back to what we were doing before. Talking to people. Making sure they're having a good time."

"You got it," she said.

They headed back into the crowd. It was getting late, and most of the kids in the crowd had disappeared, thinning the ranks somewhat. The people who were left were mostly of the "formal evening wear" variety.

In their more casual clothing, Mr. and Mrs. Beauchamp stood out in in the crowd. Angie supposed they hadn't packed for black tie occasions before setting out in their RV. She steered Walter toward the couple, noting as she did so that Alayna Karner was still nowhere to be seen. Good.

Introducing Walter to the Beauchamps might not be the wisest move, but she couldn't resist. The two of them were always saying something completely ridiculous or shocking, and Angie had just endured a series of bland conversations with possible investors. Being shocked would be a nice change of pace.

The Beauchamps were peregrinating the room, looking at the exhibits and arguing with each other. One of the NHA members—Angie could tell because of the tag—was walking with them, joining the argument with apparent interest, and even passion.

"Hello!" Angie said. "I'm so glad to see the two of you here tonight. How is everything going?"

Mr. Beauchamp said, "We're arguing about the history of the railroad. This worthy member of the Nantucket Historical Association, Mr.

Hurcum, has been explaining to us how the railroad was dismantled in 1917, but we know for a fact that a few sections of it remained in 1918."

"They were not in use," Mr. Hurcum said.

"That doesn't contradict my argument," Mr. Beauchamp said. "But I'm sure that Miss Prouty isn't interested in the fine details of the latter days of the railroad, are you, my dear?"

"I'm afraid my focus has been somewhat different," she said.

"Mrs. Beauchamp saw your little drama earlier," Mr. Beauchamp said. Mrs. Beauchamp immediately turned red in the face. "And we are glad to hear that it resulted in that Karner woman being ejected from the party."

Angie turned toward Mr. Hurcum. "Was she? I didn't know."

"She *left*," Mr. Hurcum said, "Of her own accord."

"And good thing, too," Mr. Beauchamp said. "Otherwise my little Dottie might have had a more serious argument with her."

"Charles!" Mrs. Beauchamp said.

"Well? Everyone knows that she's been following us around as we search for clues. I won't have it, and I know, given your temper, my dear, that you can't be having it either."

Mrs. Beauchamp said, "If you will excuse me," and left the group in a beeline for the ladies' room. Walter gave Angie a look, and she followed the older woman into the toilet.

Mrs. Beauchamp had torn several paper towels out of the holder and was wiping her face with them. She was clearly weeping.

"I'm sorry," Angie said, not precisely truthfully. "I didn't mean to stir up trouble."

"That man," Mrs. Beauchamp said. "He thinks it's all in good fun to humiliate me so."

"Sometimes men don't think," Angie agreed.

"All that talk about me poisoning someone, and my temper," she said. "When we were around people that we had known for decades, it was all fine and dandy. They knew it was Charles who had the hot temper, and that...that death was a terrible mistake on the part of the young lady."

Angie said something soothing, not entirely believing her, but accepting that Mrs. Beauchamp had had no part in the matter.

"But now that we're on the road all the time in the RV, it's a different matter. He won't be the least bit personable. He teases me constantly and tells me that it's my fault if I'm not happy, when I was the one who was perfectly content at home in the first place."

Mrs. Beauchamp was getting more upset rather than less. Angie said, "Do you need a place to stay for a day or two? Aunt Margery and I will put you up if you need to. I guarantee that Aunt Margery will defend you like a hellcat if he tries to butt in and stop you from having a day off."

"A day off!" Mrs. Beauchamp said. "That's what it is. Ever since the man retired, I simply haven't had a moment to myself. But no," she took a deep breath, then let it go and turned toward the mirror, wetting the paper towels and dabbing at her face. "No. I'll be all right. But I think I've had enough for the night, and I, at least, shall be going. Thank you for listening to me moan and groan about what is a perfectly ordinary situation—two grown adults who can't figure out how to get along with each other now that they're not occupied with work. That man needs a hobby, and traveling around the country in an RV isn't it. Something like joining a historical society, where he can argue all day long with someone who isn't me, would be ideal."

With an almost audible snap, Mrs. Beauchamp put herself together and strode out of the women's toilet, straight for her husband.

"Charles," she announced, "it's time to go."

"But I've—"

"Goodnight, Charles."

She pivoted and turned for the front door without looking behind her. One of the high school students who was working the coat check area had already pulled out her coat and had it ready for her.

Charles Beauchamp looked startled. He held out a hand toward Mr. Hurcum, who shook it. "I enjoyed our talk," he told the man. "Please do send me an email."

"Certainly."

"Mr. Snuock, a pleasure to meet you. I hope that your treasure hunt goes to everyone's satisfaction. Miss Prouty, lovely as always. I hope to see you for coffee of a morning."

"I'll be there if you are," she said, and refrained from advising him to stop teasing his wife so much. He already seemed to have learned his lesson. A few moments later, he had followed his wife into the night.

"What was that all about?" Walter asked.

"She was upset at being teased so much. There isn't a time that the two of them come into the bookstore and Mr. Beauchamp isn't poking at her feelings."

"Hmph," Mr. Hurcum said. "He's just bored. We old goats need something to chew on, and if it's not someone at work, it's our wives. I told him he should join the historical society. If not here, then whenever they end up. He says that he's tired of driving all over the place in the RV, but he's afraid to tell the wife for fear that he'll never hear the end of it. I told him he's a fool if he can't see that she'd do nothing of the sort…after the first year or two, anyway, and he'd deserve it if she did. Hope they get things sorted out, a couple of young people like that."

With that, Mr. Hurcum dove back into the party.

Mr. Hurcum *was* at least eighty, so the Beauchamps were at least fifteen years the younger. But Angie still had to pinch herself to restrain an audible chuckle.

Walter said, "Mr. Beauchamp did say something interesting just after you left. About the railroad."

"Oh?"

"That the railroad terminus in Sconset is still standing. It's now a private cottage."

"I didn't know that."

"Well, both of *them* did. They were talking about Tom Nevers Field, which they said was never an airport. Did you ever watch *Wings*? The old TV show?"

"No?"

"Apparently there was a fictional airplane field named Tom Nevers Field."

"But that's a park."

"That's right. Sorry, they were having one of those ongoing arguments where nobody else can get a word in edgewise and everything gets confused."

"Knowing them, I'm not surprised." But the thought was in her mind now. "Jo and Mickey and I ran into them at Sheldon's the other night. They were about to tell me a clue about the location of the painting, but they were interrupted by the sight of...well, I'm sorry to bring her name up, but Alayna Karner."

"What?"

"They said she'd been following them around all over the island." Angie frowned. Now that she knew more about Ms. Karner's past, it sounded even creepier. She grabbed Walter's arm. "Do you think we should warn them about her?"

"They're already on the lookout," Walter said. "And, if Alayna's not careful, she could end up poisoned." He laughed. "Of course Mr. Beauchamp had to start telling me all about that story about his wife, which turned out to be nothing at all. It's just the way he tells it that sounds so suspicious."

Angie rubbed the back of her neck. She was starting to run out of energy. Not that it was very late. She was just tired of being around all these people. It was the drama that was wearing her out, honestly.

"I don't see Jasper Parris anywhere," she said. "I wonder if he's still in the hospital."

As if by magic, Tabitha Crispin popped out of the crowd. She looked to be at least somewhat in her element. Nearby were Carol Brightwell, Marlee Ingersoll, and several people that Angie vaguely recognized, mostly in their early twenties.

"That poor man," Walter said. "He's been through the ringer."

"I know it."

"I feel the worst about him. Somehow, all the stress from having to deal with the treasure hunt ended up on his shoulders—and broke them."

"He'll be all right," Angie said. "I talked to him at the hospital the other day, and…"

Something occurred to her, and she drifted into silence.

"What is it?"

"Where's the rest of Reed's luggage?" she asked.

"I thought you found it."

"I found his briefcase, but it didn't have socks, underwear, or a toothbrush in it."

"It might be at the ferry station. Or his hotel."

She made a face. "I'm worrying over nothing, aren't I?"

"Possibly," he said, neither agreeing or disagreeing, but watching to see what she would do.

"Will you be all right for a moment? I need to step outside and call Detective Bailey to check on something."

"Be my guest," he said. "I'll still be here when you get back. If it weren't almost time to announce the auction results, I'd go with you. But I'm expected to present."

"Be careful," she told him. "Alayna could still be hanging around the place."

"I will."

Angie stepped out of the back door and the chill hit her immediately. So did the quiet. It was one of those dark, heavy winter evenings that feel like they'll turn to snow at any moment. In fact as she took her phone out of her tiny black purse, a snowflake did drift down in front of her—but only one.

"Hello. Detective Bailey speaking."

"Detective Bailey, this is Angie Prouty."

"Why hello, Miss Prouty. What can I do for you? I thank you for your email last night at o'dark thirty, although I have to admit that I didn't bother to read it until after the sun was up. You didn't read that whole book, did you?"

"Er," she said.

"You're quite the reader, all right. But that's not why you called, I'm sure."

"Reed's other luggage," she said. "With his toiletries and socks and whatnot. Has it turned up anywhere?"

"No, Ms. Prouty, it has not. We were able to find out where Mr. Edgerton was registered to stay for the evening." He named one of the local B&Bs within walking distance of the bookstore, but a bit out of the way of the beach where the briefcase had been found. "They hadn't seen hide nor hair of him. He did not arrive at all that evening. Incidentally, do you happen to know what kind of luggage it would be? Matching the briefcase, maybe?"

"I'm sorry. I've only ever seen him during the day in Boston. I've seen the briefcase a dozen times, but nothing else."

"Was there anything that he was in the habit of wearing, other than his watch?"

"I think he had a pair of reading glasses? And several ties that I might recognize if I saw them. He liked gray suits like the one he was wearing. And he didn't wear rings or any jewelry that I know of."

"Thank you, Ms. Prouty. I'll call the managers at the ferry stations in a minute."

She bit her lips. "Detective?"

"Yes?"

As long as she was on the phone, she might as well say something. She told him about Alayna Karner and the confrontation she had had with Walter that night, as well as what both Walter and the Beauchamps had told her.

"I'll keep an eye out for her," he promised.

Another snowflake fell in front of her. Angie was shivering like a madwoman. She went back inside.

~

The announcements had begun, although they hadn't reached the auction items yet. Beatrice Solly of the NHA was covering the preliminary announcements, most of which were both aggressively local and completely charming, like the one about the outdoor ice skating pond opening up—with hot cocoa being served every Saturday at the NHA booth—or the Santa and Mrs. Claus visit to the Whaling Museum next Thursday.

But finally it was time for the auction winners to be announced.

"First, the gift basket from Harbor Antiques," Walter said, a spotlight shining very brightly in his face at the podium that had been set up at the front of the room. He looked at the basket, all wrapped up in cellophane, then read the tag. "Containing a Nantucket salt basket of sterling silver with a cobalt blue glass lining, three vintage silk scarves, and a piece of authenticated Nantucket scrimshaw by Fredrick Myrink. The top bid, which I believe?" He glanced at Beatrice Solly, who leaned over in his ear and whispered to him. "Which we won't publicly announce in the interest of maintaining the general peace, was won by Gerald McGeury."

"Hah!" came a voice from the back of the crowd. "That'll show you, Tom Beel!"

Amused laughter echoed around the hall. Gerald McGeury came forward to collect his item.

"You'll need to pay the ladies of the NHA," Walter cautioned him. "Otherwise, I can't promise that you'll get out of here alive."

The audience chuckled. The auction announcements continued on. Angie zoned out, laughing at Walter's jokes without really listening to them. Her mind was a million miles away.

Reed had died at eleven p.m. on that tiny beach along the harbor. What had he been *doing* all that time? It was on her mind again, now that she knew he hadn't checked in at his B&B, especially when it was within walking distance. Why hadn't he come to the bookstore? Why hadn't he texted her?

It was wrong. Something about this whole situation was wrong. There were too many possible suspects. If Reed had visited someone else on the island that he knew but hadn't introduced to Angie, as Jasper had suggested, then there were approximately ten thousand suspects. If only she had access to all the information Detective

Bailey had. Would investigators from the mainland come over to help? She thought they might. It would be sooner rather than later—they might be here already, in fact. That might explain why Detective Bailey had seemed so distracted out on the beach.

She wished she had more information about Reed from Harvard. Another source of information that she couldn't access. Did he have any colleagues on the island? Old college friends? A distant cousin?

She just wanted to know what had happened. No, scratch that. She wanted justice to be done. She wanted Reed's killer caught, even if it broke her heart to find out that it was someone she knew.

Where was Reed's luggage? Had it ended up in the harbor? Had it sunk to the bottom or floated out to the ocean?

She hated this. She rubbed her forehead. Reed's death had better be over something important. A love affair, an old score to settle, a forged painting...something. If it was over the treasure hunt? She didn't know if she could take it. A painting was just a *thing*. Money shouldn't justify a death. It was a terrible thought. No, she decided, she could only take it if Reed's death was an accident or a crime of passion—something she could comprehend. A broken heart, revenge, wounded pride, the sense that one had been kicked out of a place where one belonged. Fame, even. That she could take. But not *money*.

The painting hadn't even been found.

The last prize of the night was the door prize. Reed read off a name, but no one claimed the prize. Then he drew another name. He laughed nervously. "Is this how it normally goes?" he asked Beatrice Solly. "I mean, door prizes? They're supposed to be bribes to get people to stay until the end of the night."

More laughter. Walter Snuock made for a pretty decent MC, although clearly he would never be a professional comedian.

"Just keep picking names. It's all right."

Finally he said a name Angie recognized. "Wyatt Gilmore? Is Wyatt Gilmore here?"

"I'm here." Wyatt had been standing at the back of the room. He was dressed in black jeans and his leather jacket—although black tie wasn't necessary, he did stand out amidst the formal gowns and tuxedos.

"Congratulations," Walter said heartily. "You have won…"

He picked up a basket.

"A collection of books about Nantucket," Walter said. "Including a signed copy of *The Little Grey Lady of the Sea: The Mysteries of Nantucket Island*, by our own David Dane."

The locals who were in on the joke chuckled. "David Dane" was Aunt Margery, who had written the gossipy, sensationalist book years and years ago. It had acquired a kind of local infamy.

"Unfortunately the author isn't here to greet you tonight. The other titles in the basket include…" He began listing the rest of them off as Wyatt came to the front of the room.

She had completely forgotten that she'd donated books for the gala. She'd thought they were going for the silent auction. But a lot of the silent auction items were in the three- and four-figure range; they must have decided to use her basket as the door prize so that it wouldn't stand out so much. She hadn't included anything collectible, like a signed first edition by someone famous—that would have made it something worth bidding on.

She felt sorry for herself for a count of ten, then laughed it off. Next year she'd know better what the fundraising stakes were. If they did this again, that was.

Wyatt reached the front of the room and accepted the basket. He spotted her and swerved to walk past her on the way back.

"Psst," he said. "Got a clue!"

"Good for you!" she said.

"Tell you about it in the morning," he said. "You'll be open?"

"A little late, maybe," she said. "I've had a lot of champagne. For me that is."

"You'll be there early," he said. "Just watch. You'll wake up early worried that you've overslept."

She protested that she would do no such thing, and he grinned and walked back to his place in the shadows.

The rest of the evening passed peacefully, winding down slowly but inevitably. Despite her earlier fatigue, Angie found herself reluctant to leave, especially after dancing with Walter again. Midnight came and went, and she didn't turn into her usual pumpkin self. Maybe it was just that parties on the island were both rare and *far* more entertaining than the ones in Manhattan. The band packed up and went home, and a white-haired mainlander took over the piano, playing rollicking Hoagie Carmichael tunes with a sly wink. A woman in a slinky baby-blue dress went to the coat check for a fur stole, and leaned against the piano, fluttering her eyelashes. The piano player switched to torch songs, which the woman's husky voice carried well. Then the pair switched off with Tabitha Crispin and a couple of the NHA members who sang show tunes.

Angie sang herself hoarse, her sparkly silver shoes abandoned in a corner so she could dance barefoot on the museum floor. The sperm whale skeleton overhead had acquired a Santa hat hanging off its lower jaw, as well as a few pieces of tinsel. She finally called it a night at one in the morning. Some of the NHA members looked like they were digging in. It was pointless to try to keep up with them. This party was going to last until dawn.

Walter walked her out to her car. Then he followed her home before driving across the island to Snuock Manor (which wasn't really the name of his house even though everyone on the island called it that anyway).

They must have spent five minutes kissing on her back porch. Only the fact that Aunt Margery was asleep in her room—or worse, *not* asleep in her room—kept Angie from inviting him in.

Chapter 13

THE OTHER LUGGAGE

The next morning, Angie opened the bookstore early. She had slept for a few hours, then jerked awake in the dark, panicked that she'd overslept.

Fat chance. Four-thirty a.m. seemed like nine. And once she was awake, she couldn't get back to sleep.

She laughed and got up, made a pot of coffee, and took a shower. She felt good—almost guiltily so. One of her friends had died, she hadn't solved his murder, and she'd had a good night anyway. It felt like trying to cheat fate. Surely something terrible would happen in order to balance the scales.

She whistled on the way in to work. Sunday morning. The store would either be dead because everyone was sleeping off the party, or it would be frantically busy as fate punished her for having such a good time.

It felt as though fate would have to try really hard to catch her. She was flying high as a kite.

The bookstore was fine. It hadn't burned down in the middle of the night or anything like that. Captain Parfait was happy to see her and loudly requested his breakfast, in case she had gone deaf. She unlocked the back door. No sign of pastries yet. Suddenly she remembered that Jo would be gone today.

She dialed the bakery, but hung up before Mickey could answer. He was probably going to try to do everything by himself this morning. She'd go over and pick up her own pastries this morning instead of expecting them to be delivered. Mickey and Jo didn't really need to wait on her hand and foot.

When she pulled up along the street behind the bakery, the lights were out. Worried, she walked up to the back door and cupped her hands around her face as she peered through the window.

Nobody home.

She called Mickey's number. No answer.

She called Jo's number and left a message, then drove over to Mickey's place; he was staying at his mom's house for now.

The lights were off there, too.

Where else to look? She tried to remember when she had last seen him at the party. He had been standing with Walter the last time she remembered seeing him. He hadn't been at the auction, or at least she didn't think so. Where was his car? She hadn't seen it at any of the places she'd looked for him. And it was too far to walk home. Maybe his car had died and he hadn't wanted to bother anyone. He'd walked to Jo's apartment, found her spare key, and let himself in. She'd check there next.

∼

Twenty minutes later, she was ready to tear her hair out. She had checked every place that opened early or that might have stayed open overnight. She had checked Sheldon's. She hadn't checked was Snuock Manor, but that was a half-hour drive, and why would he be there anyway? He wasn't some kind of jealous ex. He was *Mickey*.

The bakery stayed dark and his phone went to voice mail.

Angie's heart was pounding with fear. *Not again.*

Then she remembered that she hadn't checked the area around the Whaling Museum.

She wasn't sure exactly where he had parked. The downtown area was not known for its plentiful parking spaces, and locals tended to walk everywhere, even in the winter.

She drove slowly through the streets, looking for Mickey's green Honda Civic. It was past time to open the store, and she was running out of patience. Maybe it was time to call the police.

She slammed on the brakes.

She'd glimpsed a green car through a gap in the trees. It looked like it was in a church parking lot, but there was no way to reach the lot from where she was. A row of houses blocked the way. She circled around what seemed like a maze of gray houses and narrow lanes, and finally pulled into the right parking lot.

It was Mickey's car, all right, with a dozen stickers in the corners of the rear window. "Give Whirled Peas a Chance." Goofy stuff like that.

She looked inside the car, half dreading that she would find a body inside.

Nothing. Just a bunch of junk food wrappers on the floor in the back.

She looked around. If you cut through a yard, then the distance from here to the Whaling Museum would be about three blocks. Cutting through yards was exactly the kind of thing Mickey would do, too. The parking lot didn't have any cameras watching over it, unfortunately, and there was no one else parked there.

Where was he?

She drove past the bakery again. It was still closed, with no sign that Mickey had been there this morning. She called and left another message. Called Jo again. Then she drove back to the bookstore and opened up.

Her stomach was in knots. She decided not to worry about finding replacement pastries.

She saw a blinking red light on the phone next to the cash register. Voicemail? Angie couldn't remember the last time someone left a voicemail on the phone at the store—most of the locals just called her cell phone and the tourists just stopped by.

Angie pulled the phone off it's cradle and put it between her shoulder and neck, then she punched the red button and listened to the voicemail.

Angie? Hi, it's Charles Beauchamp. We weren't sure who else to call, but uh... Your friend Mickey is in the hospital. He's okay, but he slipped on some ice last night and fell. What?.... Oh, right honey... Angie, my wife wants me to tell you that we would have called earlier, but the police wanted to question us, given her record... and uh, hang on.... she also wants me to tell you...

Angie listened to the Beauchamps bicker for a full minute before the voicemail ended. She mentally kicked herself for not checking the hospital, but was happy that he was there, and not somewhere more sinister. She had lost enough friends for the year.

She dialed the hospital and after a few short minutes, she was connected with Mickey's room.

"Angie! Sorry, but I don't think I'm going to be able to get you pastries today," said Mickey into the phone.

"Mickey! I don't care about that, I'm just glad you're alright. How are you feeling? I'm coming over to see you right now."

"No, don't come. I'm totally fine, it's just a bump on the ol' noggin. I'm a little woozy, but I should be out of here in time for the lunch rush. You need to stay at the bookstore; those treasure hunters won't caffeinate themselves," said Mickey with a laugh.

∼

Wyatt Gilmore came in at about nine. He smiled at her and said, "I was wrong. You slept in."

She shook her head. "I did wake up early. Four-thirty. But a friend of mine was missing, or so I thought. I went to look for him."

"Who, the man who was playing MC last night?"

"Walter? No, this is someone else. One of the owners of the bakery. Mickey Jerritt."

"Mickey? That's terrible! Any idea where he went?"

"Yeah, I just found out he's in the hospital. He fell on ice and hit his head last night, but I don't think it's too serious. He sounds fine."

"I'm glad it was nothing worse than that," Wyatt said. Then after, after an awkward pause, he adds, "Can I tell you what I found out? I'm dying to tell someone."

"What?"

"I did some research over the last few days, and I think I have the name of the mysterious lady—the woman who would have had been given the painting. I've narrowed it down to a few different people."

"Really? Who?"

He beckoned to her, leading her away from the main floor to the doorway to the stock room as he lowered his voice. "Here's what I'm thinking. The mysterious lover of Victor Nouges must have been a woman from a prominent family. Why else would she stay? If she didn't have strong ties to the island, why wouldn't she take off to follow her lover?"

"Okay, sure. I guess I can buy that," said Angie.

"I did some data analysis on births and deaths, which got me a list of all wealthy families on the island. Wealthy families paid for birth certificates, but most working class families on the island didn't back then. Then, I did some genealogy research at the library and cross referenced it with major land purchase transactions and shipping records. Only 3 families were involved in land transactions, shipping transactions and had published birth certificates. I looked at women from those families and I narrowed it down to Eliza Snuock, Madeline Lovill, or Delilah Crispin."

"Impressive work Wyatt!"

"Thanks, I thought so." Wyatt smiled and almost blushed at the compliment.

"Eliza Snuock would be related to Walter," Angie said. "I haven't heard of any Lovills on the island. And there's a Tabitha Crispin who lives here—she works at the Chamber of Commerce."

"I've met her," Wyatt said. "Madeline Lovill lived here until midway through 1918, when she suddenly disappeared from the island, along with her maiden aunt. I tracked her down to a small town in upstate New York; she died in 1947."

"The painting disappeared in 1917," Angie said, "and if she left only a year later, it can't be her."

"Exactly," Wyatt said. "One down, two to go."

"What about the others?"

"Eliza Snuock married into the Churchill family in 1922," Wyatt said.

Angie clucked her tongue. She had only looked until 1920. "Long convalescence?"

"She broke off an engagement in 1918, but got engaged again to the same man in 1921."

"That makes sense. Especially if there was suspicion about Victor Nouges."

"She died in 1953. So it's possible, but if she married into the Churchills it's unlikely that she stayed on the island. And we're looking for someone who would have ties to the island so strong that even true love couldn't make her leave."

"Aren't you a romantic, Wyatt? But I see your point, we can rule out Eliza Snuock. And the third woman? Miss Crispin?"

"An interesting story. Her fiancé died just after World War I in an influenza outbreak. Her family was wealthy enough to support her for the rest of her life. She was known to pace along the top of the family home's widow walk until she was quite old. She passed in—wait for it—1983, aged eighty-seven."

"Wow."

"It was almost as though she were waiting for someone to return to her from the sea."

"But he never did."

"Victor Nouges never did, at any rate. Miss Crispin's family was important enough that she wouldn't have left, and we know for a fact that she never did leave, hence the articles about her on the widow walk."

"From the love letters, she did sound pretty bitter by the end. It's far from proof, but it's a great theory," Angie said, more to herself than to him. "Wait! I have something for you."

She booted up the front desk computer and pulled up the typed copy of the letter from the *An Old-Fashioned Romance* collection.

"Where did you get this?" he asked.

She explained about the book that had been in Reed's briefcase.

"You're right, she does sound bitter," Wyatt agreed after reading. "Well, the next step is to start digging into what properties the different families owned around the island. If I can build a matrix of the Crispin's land ownership, I can narrow down the possible locations of the painting."

"That is easier said than done," Angie said. "the land records aren't perfectly accurate here on the island."

"True but...I guess I'm enjoying the challenge" he shifted his weight from foot to foot. "This has turned from a quest to find a painting so I can make enough money to live on, into a kind of working job interview. I met with some of Mickey's friends—"

"Mickey mentioned something about that, how's it going?" asked Angie.

"Actually, it's going great. I may have found my second career, but it's early yet. How's your investigation going? You know, with Reed?"

Angie sighed. "I don't know. I'm hitting dead end after dead end. I'm so tired. I probably just need another cup of coffee."

She picked up her cup of coffee and took a sip, the taste of the coffee was wrong, like wood chip soup. Angie spit it out immediately in the trash can under the counter.

"I think this is your culprit, here," said Wyatt. He was pointing to Captain Parfait, who stood next to a pencil sharpener that had been overturned and dumped the pencil shavings into Angie's mug.

Captain Parfait jumped down and curled up unapologetically around Angie's leg.

Angie stopped. Several things had just fallen into place.

"Wyatt…"

"What is it?"

"What if…someone put something in Jasper's coffee?"

He frowned at her. He wasn't following along.

"In his coffee?"

"I delivered coffee to the Chamber of Commerce that day, because their coffeemaker had failed."

"Okay…"

"So here's what I think happened: Reed arrives on the island and stops at the Chamber of Commerce. Because the computer is down, he writes his information on a piece of paper for Jasper to type in later, when the computer is working. Jasper doesn't see him—he's trying to fix the computer. Instead, Reed is met by someone else, someone I know has been around the office all day."

"Who, Marlee Ingersoll? She's the college kid, right? Why would she be involved in this?"

"No," Angie said. "I think Reed suspected that the Monet was a forgery. What if Reed was right, what if the painting is a *fake*? What if someone drugged Jasper so they could stop Reed from uncovering the forged painting?"

"No," Wyatt said.

"Yes. Reed had done his research. He noticed Tabitha's name on the list of employees at the Chamber of Commerce. He did the same research that you did and came up with the same list of names you did. How hard would it be to match the names up?"

"Does she have an alibi?"

"She *says* she left at five, along with everybody but Jasper, who had taken the computer into the back room to work on it where the lights were better. But what if she stayed long enough that Reed came in, gave her his information, and…said something that he shouldn't have?"

"Like what?"

"Like anything. 'Did you know you had an ancestor on the island back during the time of the mysterious lovers?' That's all it would take. A slip of the tongue."

"And then what? She kills him to keep the forgery under wraps? He didn't die until eleven, or so I heard. Unless that's not true."

"No, I heard that from Detective Bailey." She made a face. "Oh, Wyatt. I've been an idiot. Probably because I'm not a professional detective or a medical doctor. But it's just the kind of thing that would be in a classic mystery, so I shouldn't have missed it at all. Reed was found in the harbor in December."

"So?"

"So rigor mortis might not have set in yet."

"I would have thought it would have set in quickly, given that it was so cold."

"No, rigor mortis isn't about the body hardening because it's cold. It happens because the muscle tissues are breaking down. Heat speeds up rigor mortis, because decay is sped up. I read enough mystery novels—I should have this memorized," Angie said. "Anyway, if it's cold, the body doesn't go into rigor mortis right away, because the cell walls are still intact. If you froze a body quickly enough, it probably never would go into rigor mortis, or at least until you thawed it out."

"So?"

"So the people who would normally do autopsies aren't available. The morgue isn't ready at the new hospital location yet. Which left the autopsy to someone at the funeral home who's less experienced. It's the kind of thing that would have gotten caught on the mainland, but we just don't have the expertise to handle it here."

"And the bloodstain? The murder weapon?"

"Tabitha came into Sheldon's Shuckery at six fifteen," Angie said. "I *saw* her. She came in right before I did. The Shuckery is along the harbor, although you can't get a clear view of the part of the beach where we found the bloodstain. Reed comes in, she takes down his information, Reed drops some hint about forgery and that he knows that her ancestress is involved, and then leaves. She follows him.

"He panics and, realizing what she's capable of, tries to lead her towards the police station. She finally catches up to him along the beach. They argue. She hits him with something—any blunt object would do. To be charitable, let's say that she didn't kill him on purpose. Maybe she was angry and it happened in the heat of the moment.

"Reed falls down dead. She panics, drags the body into the water and shoves it out into the current. She does the same thing with Reed's luggage. Then there's the briefcase. Even though it was still early in the evening, it's December, so it would have been too dark to read the book and documents. She can't risk finding a streetlight and reading them there—she needs to get somewhere very public, very soon. So she buries the briefcase, possibly with the intention of coming back for it later. The cleanup doesn't take long, but like I said, it's dark, so she doesn't spot the patch of blood above the tide line. She brushes out the drag marks and lets the tide do the rest.

"Then she goes to the Shuckery. Okay, it's not the world's most airtight alibi. She says she left the Chamber of Commerce at five, then arrives at the Shuckery at six fifteen and hangs around until closing time with a couple of other people from the office. When asked what she was doing between those times, she says she was at home taking a shower. But it works out, because the doctor doing the autopsy isn't all that experienced at it, and puts the time of death at eleven p.m., when she was clearly at the Shuckery, having a great time. She only needed to get lucky twice. Her first bit of luck was that nobody saw her following Reed out of the Chamber of Commerce, or at least nobody *from the island* saw her. Any number of tourists could have seen her, thought nothing of it, and gone back to the mainland by now. Her second bit of luck was the doctor calling the time of death for the wrong time."

Wyatt said, "I'm all for a good theory, but where's the data? It's a big accusation you would be making, and while it does sound pretty plausible, you don't have proof."

Angie frowned. It felt like the case melted in front of her, dissolving like a wet paper towel into mush.

"I don't," she sighed. "You're right. I have a theory. I don't have anything I can give to Detective Bailey, and I don't have anything that could be presented before a judge."

"Which means what?"

"That I need to collect evidence that shows, beyond a shadow of a doubt, that Tabitha Crispin murdered Reed Edgerton."

Chapter 14

THE PURLOINED LETTER

The first step was to talk to Jasper and find out whether it was possible that Tabitha had been in the office any later than five p.m. If, for example, Jasper had been in and out of the back room with the computer and hadn't seen her there at all, then Angie needed to ditch her theory completely. But if he had been so involved with the computer that he wouldn't have noticed anyone coming into the office—either Tabitha *or* Reed—then she would proceed to step two.

She didn't know where Jasper lived off the top of her head, but fortunately (or unfortunately), he was still in the hospital. He was willing to talk to her.

"You're off early," he said.

"I left Aunt Margery in charge of the bookstore," she said. She'd made a rare exception to her rule to let her great-aunt arrive at the store whenever she saw fit. Aunt Margery had shown up at ten-thirty, which was practically unheard of.

Jasper waved his hand at the three books she'd brought him to read.

"The art book was nothing much," he said. "Too many snippets of gossip that were not-quite-true, and not enough paintings. Only a single Monet, would you believe it?"

It was one of the books that Reed had picked out for her as a fun coffee-table art book. She gave Jasper a thin smile, unable suddenly to say anything. He missed her reaction and kept talking.

"The Jack Reacher put me to sleep," he said, "I tried to relate to the characters but I couldn't. I just can't see myself as a six-foot-tall ex-military cop who never washes his clothes."

"Don't you enjoy the romance of the freedom of the road, with nothing to tie you down?"

"Oh, no," he said. "Leave that for the idiot motorcycle-riders in their cool black leathers and no pension plan."

"What about the romance?" she asked. It was beginning to sound like she selected those three books so carefully without managing to find anything he actually liked.

"Oh, that one I liked," he said. "Predictable, of course, but I chuckled at it most of the way through."

"I'm glad you liked one of the books, at least."

He flashed her a smile. "I didn't mean to criticize your tastes. I just wanted to talk about the books with someone who would understand."

"It's been a stressful day," she admitted. "I'm not as quick on the uptake as I usually am. Witty banter will resume by the time you're out of the hospital, I promise."

"Most appreciated. Did you bring anything else for me?"

She hadn't; she had been in such a rush to get out of the bookstore that it hadn't even crossed her mind. She apologized and offered to run back and pick something out for him. He shook his head. "I'll see if the hospital library has more by that romance writer. My mind isn't up for *War and Peace*, honestly, or even a Ken Follett. But if you didn't bring any other books, why did you come?"

She apologized again, feeling quite warm in the face. She really should have thought before she'd come.

"To be honest," she said finally, "I'm here to ask you a few questions about the night of Reed's murder. That is, let me back up. Detective Bailey, at least, is convinced that it's a case of murder."

"He's come to question me twice," Jasper said.

"And...he's a little tight with his information," Angie said.

"As he should be."

"As he should be," she agreed, "but I'm too nosy to let it go. So I came to ask you about the night of the murder."

"Yes?" he asked cautiously.

"What time did you take the computer into the back room to work on it?"

"After the others left, about five p.m."

"And you're sure they left."

He frowned at her. "As I said, I went into the back room to work on the computer. They said they were leaving."

"But you didn't check."

"Why would I?"

She bit the inside of her cheek for a moment. "If someone had come in, would you honestly have heard it? I know you have to claim you would have heard them for the sake of your job, but you were working on the computer in the other room pretty intently."

He chuckled softly. "Angie, that's what's known as a leading question. You want me to say that I wouldn't have heard it if someone came in. Why? Do you think that one of the other employees stayed late for some reason, ran into Reed, and...what? Hit him over the head and dragged him out to the bay? It's only two blocks to the wharf, after all, and who knows? The murderer and victim might have been lucky and gone unseen by the tourists."

"Something like that," Angie admitted.

Jasper shook his head. "None of the people working at the Chamber of Commerce could have done it, Angie. I *know* them. This isn't some kind of game. You can't just make accusations like that."

"That's why I'm asking you first," she said. "If you had gone out to the front room and saw there was no one there, I'd just drop it."

"But?"

"But you didn't. And now there's another piece of, well, I don't know if you could call it evidence, but a pretty persuasive coincidence that suggests someone in particular."

"Who?"

Angie shook her head. "It's confidential."

"It's about the painting, isn't it?" he said.

"It's confidential."

He rolled his eyes. "All right. In the interest of strict accuracy, I suppose that it's *remotely* possible that I might not have heard someone come into the front office, even though it is my *job* to step out front if someone comes through the door. But I'd like to stress that I don't think it happened, and that I would have heard it regardless."

"Another question," Angie said. "When was the last cup of coffee that you had that night?"

He blinked at her. "The last cup of coffee?"

"Humor me."

"I don't know. About eleven or so, after I saw the police lights flashing along the streets."

Angie thought about the Chamber of Commerce building. The "front" of the office would face toward the wharf and the lighthouse. The police station was on Fairgrounds Road, and any route that the police would have taken between the police station and the lighthouse would have passed near the building. But the back room didn't have a window.

She said as much.

"Oh, by then I'd moved to the front of the office," he said. "The CPU fan wasn't working, which was part of what was going wrong with the computer. It was overheating. I took the whole thing apart and blew it out, then replaced the fan. I happened to have one on hand in the storeroom, actually pulled it out of another computer that had failed earlier. But once I had the computer up and running again, about seven or so, I moved it back into the front room. Of course, the fan was only the first of the many, many problems I had to fix."

Angie remembered passing the office at one-thirty that morning and seeing Jasper inside at the front desk, and she nearly slapped herself.

"So you were in the back room from approximately five until seven, and while you're pretty sure you would have heard someone come in, you wouldn't swear to it."

"Essentially, yes. But it feels like you're trying to press me toward an answer that isn't quite true."

"I'm sorry," she said.

"But you think I shouldn't be protecting whoever it is that you suspect, is that right?"

She didn't answer.

"What about the coffee?" he asked.

"What time did you become ill?"

"What time did I collapse? I don't know. Not long after I finished with the computer."

"By nine a.m.?"

"I'd have to check to see when I was admitted, but I think so. Maybe a little earlier or later."

"Did you rinse out the coffee pot after you poured all the coffee out of it?"

"No, I just left it for the girls in the morning."

The pots had been rinsed out when she'd checked them, Angie remembered, but she'd cleaned them out again with a sponge brush and some dish soap before she'd run them through the dishwasher. So someone had bothered to clean them before she'd picked them up.

"Did the coffee taste unusual in any way?"

"No. It was just coffee."

"Would you tell me if it wasn't?"

"No one at the Chamber of Commerce killed Reed Edgerton," he said stubbornly.

"Then who did?"

"How should I know? One of the other tourists. They found out that he had some kind of clue and decided to off him before he was able to take the prize money. Wyatt Earp—sorry, Gilmore. He seems like a likely suspect."

Angie said, "Do you have anything on him?"

"No! I don't have anything on anyone! I'm just—"

He stopped.

"I think you should go now," he said. "I'm not supposed to get upset right now because of my heart. And I am."

She left.

She couldn't say conclusively that Tabitha Crispin wasn't the murderer, and there was no way to determine whether she had done something to the coffee to make Jasper ill. If her suspicions were correct, then she had wanted to get him out of the office in order to either get rid of the paper slips before he could enter them, or to either hide or move something in the office.

The next step would be to check the Chamber of Commerce office. But that might mean coming into contact with Tabitha herself.

If she handed this over to Detective Bailey, she wouldn't have to do it herself.

She chewed on her lip as she thought it over, and then she drove back to the Chamber of Commerce. As she circled the block, looking for a parking space, she suddenly jerked the wheel and drove toward the boat rental place along the beach.

She pulled into the first empty spot she spotted and checked her phone for directions to the police station. The bright line marking the nearest route between the Chamber of Commerce and the police station passed right in front of the boat rental shop.

Underneath her heavy jacket, Angie felt the hair on her arms stand up straight.

Reed hadn't wanted to lead trouble straight to the bookstore. *He'd been heading for the police.* Had he called them? She dialed Detective Bailey but he wasn't available, so she left a message asking him to call her. She wasn't sure how to phrase her request, anyway. "Tell me if Reed called the police office" sounded too direct—he'd look into the matter and tell her that he couldn't say anything. "Was there any possibility that a call could have been made to the police office at about five forty-five, and get cut off?" Same problem, and phrased so that Detective Bailey's nose would start wriggling with interest. He might have already known the answer and wasn't willing to tell her. She didn't know.

How was she going to get the proof she needed? Or to at least get Detective Bailey to admit that he already had enough proof?

She didn't know what to do next. Talking to Jasper had left a bad taste in her mouth. She could go back to the funeral home and question the doctor who had called Reed's time of death. That might work.

A big RV rolled slowly past her and turned toward the bookstore parking lot. The Beauchamps. Angie waved from the window of her car, and to her surprise they stopped and waited for her.

Angie pulled up alongside them and leaned out the window of her Golf just as Mr. and Mrs. Beauchamp were climbing out of the stopped RV. They both looked…unusually happy. Mrs. Beauchamp practically jumped out of her skin when she saw Angie, and slammed the RV door behind her.

Mr. Beauchamp stood, smiling in front of the RV and looked back and forth from Angie to his wife, from his wife to Angie, as if waiting for Mrs. Beauchamp to say something.

"Mr. Beauchamp, Mrs. Beauchamp," Angie said. "How are you?"

Mrs. Beauchamp said, "Oh, Angie. We are just terrific."

Mr. Beauchamp gave her a kiss on the cheek.

"You see, Angie," he said with his arm around his wife, "we had a long talk and realized we are both quite sick of this RV and the travel. Even though we both pretended to like it, turns out the Beauchamps are a stationary pair, not meant to wonder. We are headed out on the ferry right after we wrap a little business with this treasure hunt."

The Beauchamps were positively bubbling. Angie had never seen them like this, it was all so… sweet. They were usually so harsh to each other, but I guess being stuck in an RV behind a coffee shop will do that to anyone.

"Well, I guess I'm happy for you two. What business do you need to wrap up before you leave?"

It was Mrs. Beauchamp who began to explain. "We've found the painting," she said. "We've both seen it."

Angie's eyes widened.

"It's beautiful," Mrs. Beauchamp said, "and quite safe where it is, as long as…well, as long as a hundred different things that might go wrong, don't. I think it should be made public. Charles doesn't—he thinks we should leave well enough alone."

"Dottie was the one who worked it out," Mr. Beauchamp said proudly. "My Dot."

"I went through piles and piles of old hospital records," Mrs. Beauchamp said. "Most of them on microfiche. Not all births and deaths are listed in the newspaper, you know, especially when there's a question as to the father."

Angie smashed her palms into her eyes. "Why didn't I think of that?"

"You wouldn't have known, dear," Mrs. Beauchamp said. "Times were different then. It's not the terrible shame to be born out of wedlock now that it was then."

"I still feel like I should have caught that," Angie said.

Mrs. Beauchamp gave her a slightly smug look. Angie couldn't blame her.

"I found the name of a young woman who gave birth to a child, and it struck me," Mrs. Beauchamp said. "The name given was 'Katherine Doleur.'"

"Katherine...Doleur? Sadness? Grief?"

"Yes. In French, of course. And Katherine's after Saint Katerina, the one who was tortured on a spiked wheel."

"Ah," Angie said.

"Exactly. A babe was born to her, a little girl who unfortunately died before leaving the hospital, or at least that's what the records show. The trail on the baby goes dead."

"But the mother?"

"Left behind an address, to a house on Sconset that wasn't a house at all, but the Sconset terminal for the old railroad. It's a rental cottage now; me and Charles rented it for a night and searched the place. The painting is under glass, behind a fine calligraphed piece of old vellum that explains the history of the house."

"Only place it could have been," Mr. Beauchamp said. "The purloined letter, right? It's always the last place you look."

It's always the last place you look because once you find what you're looking for, you stop looking! Angie thought to herself.

Angie didn't have the heart to mention that the painting might be a fake. "That's unbelievable!" she said instead. "When are you going to claim the prize?"

Come to think of it, would the prize still be offered if the lost Monet turned out to be a forgery? She hoped so, for their sake.

But the Beauchamps both stared at her.

"We don't want the prize money," Mr. Beauchamp said.

"Why?"

The Beauchamps looked at each other. This time it was Mr. Beauchamp who explained.

"Angie, this whole treasure hunt – the whole thing with the RV, this was about re-connecting for Dot and I. After our talk last night, we finally did that. I guess we found what we were searching for on this wonderful little island. The painting seems... better left for someone who is still searching." He said.

"Wow," said Angie. "Well, congratulations anyway. What condition was the painting in when you saw it?"

"Fine condition. We left it there, just screwed the frame back onto the wall and touched up the paint a bit. Took five minutes at the hardware shop to match the paint chip, no questions asked."

"Well, congratulations, again" Angie said. "When do you leave the island?"

"Well, we want to make sure Mr. Jerritt is all right. He was in pretty bad shape last night."

"When we found him, we both switched back into parent mode I guess. That was the first step in reconnecting. I suppose we want to make sure he's alright before we leave. Just seems like the right thing to do," said Mrs. Beauchamp.

"He was unconscious," Mr. Beauchamp said carefully. "We drove him toward the hospital, and then he started moaning things out loud, babbling about killers and murders and who was to blame. We couldn't make sense of it really—that boy really whacked his head when he fell."

Angie nodded and wondered to herself if Mickey was in worse shape than he had let on.

~

As the Beauchamps drove away, Angie stood there not knowing what to do with herself. The Beauchamps had reconciled, the painting had been found, but no prize money had been claimed.

Before she had time to think, she spotted an old green Land Rover pulling up to her. Walter.

He got out and went over to her.

"Angie, what are you doing out here?" he asked

"Well, I went to see Jasper at the Hospital and then I ran into the Beauchamps, and now I guess I'm out in the cold talking to you."

Walter walked over an embraced her.

They stood in the parking lot and held each other. Then Angie checked her phone. No calls from Jo, but one from Detective Bailey.

She called him back.

"Hello, Ms. Prouty. Sounds like you've been busy. You haven't happened to solve the mystery yet, have you?"

It caught her by surprise.

"Not...quite?" she said.

He chuckled. "You're spinning your wheels too. No shame in that. Did you still need something? Or was it about the Beauchamps and Mickey Jerritt?"

"Something else," she said. There was no clever way to say this that wouldn't come out all wrong, so she just spat it out. "Detective, is there any way if you can find out whether Reed Edgerton called 911 on the evening or afternoon that he died? Or have you already checked that, and I'm barking up the wrong tree?"

"We did check his phone records, Ms. Prouty. And there are no 911 calls listed to that number."

"Oh." She blew out her cheeks. "Then I am spinning my wheels."

"How is that?"

"I happened to be driving along Washington Street and realized that if I were going to go more or less straight from the Chamber of Commerce to the police station, it would be along that route."

"That's true. And you think that if Reed knew he was being followed, he would have tried to call 911."

"Yes. Because if he didn't have his phone, he wouldn't have known which way to go, probably, and if he did have his phone, why didn't he call 911? If he wasn't being followed, why would he go to the police station? Why not the bookstore?"

"No idea, Ms. Prouty."

"Sorry to bother you."

"No trouble."

She didn't tell him about the painting. She hadn't told *anyone* about the painting yet, not even Aunt Margery or Walter. She wasn't sure what to do about it. Was it fair to give away the location of the painting? Should she let the mystery play out on its own or help someone who, as the Beauchamps put it, was 'still searching for something?' What if it it *did* turn out to be a fake?

She didn't need to make a decision at that exact moment.

Walter said, "It sounds like you had the murderer almost worked out."

"Almost," she said. "But the information didn't go the way I wanted it to."

"Dead end?"

"Not quite. I'm at the point where I have a suspicion but no proof one way or another."

"Want to tell me about it?"

She sized him up.

"Or do you think I've already done enough damage?" he joked, his face strained enough to show that he wasn't really joking.

"I think you have a lot on your mind. You're worried about the treasure hunt and maybe you even blame yourself a little for Reed's death. I'm confident that I'm right, but what if I'm wrong? This person..." She looked around the parking lot, chewing on her cheek again. "...is a local. If I'm wrong, then that person's entire life might be tainted with even just the suspicion of murder."

"I don't like that you're involved," he said. "I don't want to limit you, or tie you down, or tell you what to do, but I don't like it. It seems like this person must have murdered Reed to silence him. And here you are, stirring things up even more. It might seem like it would be easier just to silence you, too."

"I know," she said. "But if I just sit on my hands and do nothing when I'm so close, I won't be able to live with myself. Murderers need to come to justice, and puzzles shouldn't go unsolved."

He shook his head. "I just worry about you, Angie."

She suddenly felt terrible for not telling him about the painting. But she still hadn't made up her mind regarding that just yet. She needed a minute to sit down and think. To sort through what she wanted. What *would* be justice in this situation? How could it be carried out without hurting too many people?

And now that she knew that Reed hadn't called 911, what should she do next to prove that Tabitha had murdered him?

"Ugh, it's too cold to be standing around out here," she said. "Let's go into the bookstore at least."

"Why don't I take you somewhere else?" he asked. "Give you time to calm down from everything hitting you at once, at least?"

"You're just as bad off as I am, if not worse," she reminded him.

"Good grief, stop trying to out-helpful me," he said.

She stuck out her tongue at him, grabbed his arm, and started leading him toward the bookstore.

"I would have thought it would be closed," Walter said.

"Aunt Margery came in early to cover for me."

"That's a first, isn't it?"

"Well, maybe not a first, but certainly in the low single digits."

They entered through the back door and took off their coats. Not only was Aunt Margery at the checkout desk, but Janet Hennery had come in early. They both waved at her.

Janet approached them bearing cups of coffee. "What a morning! How was the hospital?"

"Fine," Angie said, fibbing a bit. She wasn't in the mood to get into her unsettling conversation with Jasper just yet."

"Is it true that the Beauchamps murdered Reed and attacked Mickey, and that's why they are in such a rush to get off the island?" asked a random treasure hunter from the crowd at the bookstore.

The café went quiet. Everyone was looking in Angie's direction, waiting to hear her response.

Standing next to the counter, waiting to pay for a latte, was Tabitha Crispin.

She looked *extremely* curious to see what Angie would say, too.

Chapter 15

UNWELCOME

Clearly, Angie was *not* going to get a minute to think about the situation before talking. The bookstore had fallen into an expectant hush.

She couldn't locate the person who asked the question among the crowd, but it didn't matter. From the faces in front her, everyone had the same question. There was a lot to clear up.

"The Beauchamps found Mickey, and he's in the hospital. That part is true, but they didn't attack him. He slipped and fell on the ice last night. He has a pretty bad concussion. His sister Jo's on the way back from the mainland. Do *not* call her at this time. When she finds out more about how Mickey's doing she'll call me, and I'll pass the information along to everyone here."

"What about the Beauchamps?" someone asked.

"First of all, they definitely didn't kill Reed. They are leaving the island because they are no longer participating in the treasure hunt. Turns out they don't like traveling in an RV and hunting for treasure.

They are good people, and that's all the news I have for you right now. If you want more you'll just have to wait like everyone else for the gossip to make its way around town."

A few people laughed. Angie took a sip of her coffee.

"Any updates about the search for the painting? Supposedly the Beauchamps figured out where the painting was."

"Supposedly there's a lot of gossip going around," Angie said. "Please, I'm sorry. This morning is a bit of a mess. We're doing the best we can. Please be patient and wait for some actual news. Thank you."

She turned on her heel and walked onto the sales floor, making her normal rounds. She hoped that people would get the hint. Most of them did, but some of them stopped to ask her the same questions she'd just answered, as if they thought she'd come up with a different answer, just for them.

It was annoying. She tried to keep an even tone and a smile on her face.

Then every hackle on the back of her neck went up.

She turned around. Alayna Karner was walking up to her from behind, eyes slitted and narrow.

"Hello, Ms. Karner," Angie said.

"You."

"Yes, me."

Alayna Karner started ranting at her as if they were in one of the daytime soaps Angie used watched with Aunt Margery when she was a kid. It was the classic "you're trying to steal my man from me" speech, with a little "he wasn't your man to begin with" thrown in for good measure.

Angie sighed and said, "Ms. Karner, are you aware that Walter Snuock is standing right behind you this moment, listening to every ugly word you say?"

Alayna turned around and saw Walter standing over her, a frown pinching his eyebrows together.

"Alayna," he said. "You have to leave me alone. We're not dating. We're not ever going to date. After the behavior you have shown me and my friend, I'm never going to speak to you again. I'll have a restraining order put on you if I have to."

Angie couldn't see Alayna's face, but she could see Alayna lift her chin and straighten her back. "I'll never give up on you."

Walter looked hopelessly over Alayna's shoulder at Angie.

Angie said, "You'll need to leave my store, Ms. Karner. Right now."

"I don't—"

"This building is Mr. Snuock's property, and I'm the current leaseholder," Angie said. "I can call the police, and they *will* remove you from the premises. If necessary, I'll have you charged with trespassing."

She had no idea whether that would fly, but it sounded pretty convincing. She pulled her phone out of her pocket and dialed the police station, but didn't hit the call button yet.

"Are you going to leave, or will I have to have you removed?"

Alayna opened her mouth to respond. Then Wyatt Gilmore and another man appeared on either side of Alayna Karner.

Wyatt said, "You need to leave. You're not welcome here."

"I don't have to—"

Wyatt took a step closer, and puffed out his chest. It was clear he would remove her if she didn't leave of her own accord. Angie made a mental note that Wyatt was officially on the list of good people in this world.

Alayna stamped her foot, and grunted. She stared down Wyatt for a moment before storming out of the bookstore.

Aunt Margery locked the front door and stood there with her arms crossed.

Outside, Alayna Karner stood and stared through the shop windows, straining to see inside...straining to see Walter. Angie pushed him behind a bookshelf and out of sight.

Seeing this, the woman's face turned ugly. She bent down and picked up a rock, then threw it at the big plate-glass window in front of the café area.

Crack!

For a second, Angie thought the glass would crack and shatter into a thousand pieces—but it was too heavy for that. Instead, a chip of glass popped out of the sheet. That was it.

Angie laughed—what a tempest in a teapot!

But Aunt Margery had her phone out. "Hello? This is Margery Prouty at the Pastries & Page-Turners bookshop, and I'd like to report an incident of vandalism, by a Ms. Alayna Karner. K-a-r-n-e-r. Yes, she's still in front of the bookstore."

Crack!

Another stone hit a window. This time it was the smaller one in the front door—the one right in front of Aunt Margery's face.

Angie shouted "No!" and started running for the front of the store. Then came to a grinding halt. Walter had caught the back of her sweater one fist. A split second later, he had her by the arm.

"Don't give her the satisfaction," he said. "She's the one who ends up in jail, not you."

By then, Aunt Margery had stepped away from the door. This time, the glass *did* shatter, first crazing from the impact point out to the edges of the glass, then sloughing out of the doorframe with a sound like snow sliding off a roof. *Shhhhhhussssss!*

"Yes, she's just broken a window," Aunt Margery said calmly into the phone.

Through the broken window, they could hear sirens fast approaching. It was only a few blocks to the police office from the bookstore, after all.

Wyatt Gilmore stood by the side of Aunt Margery. Alayna had picked up another rock from the street—a loose cobblestone this time. If *that* hit anyone, it could be deadly.

She pulled an arm back and took aim.

"Stop!" shouted a voice from the street. "Ms. Karner, you're under arrest."

Alayna turned, threw the rock down the street toward the voice, and started running in the other direction. A second later, two uniformed police offers crossed in front of the plate-glass window, running after her.

Walter said, "I am *not* defending her this time. I don't care how much money her family throws at me. Good luck to whoever gets her after this."

Angie put a hand over her face. Her heart was racing. It could have been worse. It could have been *so* much worse., but she was still feeling shaken. She sucked in a deep breath, and Walter put an arm around her.

She heard the crunch of glass. Janet had come forward with a dustpan, broom, and trash can, and was scooping up the glass from the floor.

Angie wiped her eyes and untangled herself from Walter's arm. "It'll be just a moment until we have the front door clear," she announced. "If you need to step out right away, please feel free to use the back door. A huge thank you to Mr. Gilmore for *persuading* Ms. Karner to leave the bookstore."

Walter started applauding. "Thank you, Mr. Gilmore."

"No problem," Wyatt said from the other side of the room.

Suddenly, everything seemed clear, and Angie knew exactly what she needed to do...except for one thing. She still needed proof that Tabitha Crispin had killed Reed. Once she had that, everything would fall into place.

Chapter 16

ONE LAST PIECE OF EVIDENCE

The customers began to sort themselves out. The casual tourists either left via the back door or returned to their book browsing. A few of them even helped Janet clean up the worst of the glass. Angie dragged the shop vac out from the back room and went over the area with it, even vacuuming Aunt Margery's pant legs, socks, and shoes.

Tabitha Crispin lingered in the store. After Angie had put the fires out, as it were, she came up to the café counter and said, "I'm sorry, Tabitha, you've been standing here for at least ten minutes. Do you need something?"

"Do you have a minute?"

"I do," Angie said. "Would you like to step into the back room?"

How she managed to say it in even a relatively normal voice, she had no idea. She hoped that she was keeping her true feelings off her face, too, but it was probably too much to ask for.

Once in the stock room and out of sight of the others, Tabitha said, "I found something in the office."

Angie blinked. She hadn't been sure what to expect from the conversation, but it wasn't this. "What?"

Tabitha took out a plastic freezer bag, the kind that you can press to seal. *They make great evidence bags,* Angie thought. Inside was a piece of paper about three by five inches. It was partially crumpled. Tabitha put it on the desk with the ordering computer and pressed it flat, then handed it to Angie.

Name: Reed Edgerton

Address: 33 Copley Street, Cambridge, MA 02138.

Email...

And so on.

The two women looked at each other. Angie felt her veins turn to ice, which was something that she'd read about before but never really experienced. Her teeth literally chattered. But she couldn't even begin to guess what the paper meant.

Tabitha whispered, "I found it behind the recycle bin when I was bagging everything up to go out tomorrow morning. It's a registration card."

Angie felt as though she were about to start shouting. Or vomiting.

Tabitha said, "I put it in a baggie so it wouldn't get any more fingerprints on it. Was that right?"

"You should...take that to the police, Tabitha. You shouldn't have shown it to me first. You should have gone straight to the cops."

Tabitha looked pityingly at her. "Reed was your friend, Angie. I owe it to you to find out what you want to do."

"I want you to go to the police station and turn that over to Detective Bailey."

Tabitha nodded. "As soon as I flattened it out I knew that I'd made a mistake. I shouldn't have touched it."

"Let's just take it to the police," Angie said. "We can talk about this later, okay?"

"Okay. You'll come with me?"

"I'll come with you," Angie said. They walked out to Angie's car, which was closer, Angie telling Walter and Aunt Margery that she would be right back.

Her thoughts were a mess. What did this mean? She could barely grasp the possibilities. Did this change everything? Or was this an effort on Tabitha's part to frame someone else?

Whether the killer is Tabitha or not, she thought, *at least she won't kill me while I'm driving.*

Probably.

∾

Tabitha was still telling and retelling her story to Detective Bailey when Angie left the police station.

Her head was spinning. If Tabitha was the killer, why was she being so cooperative with the Detective? Why had she brought the clue to Angie in the first place?

A vibration in her purse interrupted her thoughts. Her phone was ringing.

"Hello?"

"Is this Ms. Agatha Prouty of Nantucket?" said the deep male voice on the other end of the voice.

"Yes, who is this?" She asked.

"I'm a friend of the Baker? He said you would know who we are."

Angie's fear dissipated, these were Mickey's friends, the tech guys.

"Yes, I'm a friend of Mi... the Baker. Do you have the information for me?" She asked.

"We do."

Angie sat down on the curb right there and pulled out her notebook. She took furious notes as the man talked. The conversation was a flood of information, and Angie couldn't sort it out as he talked. She would just have to analyze her notes later.

As the conversation ended, Angie thanked them for the help. "I can't tell you how grateful I am for the help. This whole world of forging and stealing art, I'm all very new to this."

"Well Ms. Prouty, even the thieves like us are artists in a way. It's like Picaso said: Good artists copy, great artists steal."

Angie's head almost exploded as puzzle pieces started falling into place her head.

The lost Monet probably *wasn't* a fake after all, but there was definitely a forger on the island.

She needed to get to the hospital. Now.

When she arrived, she flew past the check in station, and took the stairs two at a time until she got to Mickey's floor.

"Mickey, thank goodness you are okay," she said between gasps.

"Angie, of course I'm okay. Better than okay, they are discharging me any minute now." Mickey smiled and waved a cup of green Jello at her, "No more Jello!"

His smile faded as he realized this wasn't just a friendly check in.

"Ang, what's wrong?"

"Mickey, I spoke to your friends, the internet guys."

"The internet guys?" he repeated with evident amusement.

"You know who I mean. The hackers. They were very helpful."

"Glad to hear it. What did they say?"

"You know that Reed had all kinds of information about forged paintings in his briefcase right?"

"Sure."

"Turns out a lot of art changes hands on the black market. In fact, many mafia families deal in art, especially ones with ties to Europe. Through the mafia you can get stolen pieces or original art without paying taxes, stuff like that. Interestingly enough, many of the so-called legitimate paintings in circulation now are actually forgeries. The mafia buys forgeries and passes them off as real."

Mickey nodded, but was clearly not following.

"Wouldn't people come after the mafia once they found out a painting was fake?" he asked.

"Sometimes, but according to your friends, the forger always takes the fall. If a painting is discovered to be fake, the mafia finds the forger, or their family, and serves them up to the buyer on a silver platter."

"So why would anyone sell a forgery to the mafia? If they know they are going to get found out…"

"Why does anyone deal with the mob? Desperation. Money. If you forge a painting that's not in circulation, you might get away with it. According to your friends, the profile of someone who sold a forged painting to the mob is someone who was artistically gifted, desperate for money, and has a family that's easy to leverage."

Mickey's eyes went wide.

"You know, I heard the nurses talking about a patient here who drew the most amazing pictures. They said they had never seen anything so beautiful on a napkin…"

"…or a tie perhaps?" offered Angie.

"Jasper!?" whispered Mickey.

"Let's get you out of here and go find out."

She left Mickey in the discharge lounge awaiting his paperwork. He was his same goofy, charismatic self even after his head injury. He had already promised the hospital staff cupcakes in the shape of the island, and then he'd started cracking jokes with the other patients. By the time Angie slipped out, Mickey had the whole room laughing.

She needed to see Jasper one more time, just to be sure. He was only one floor up, and she promised herself she would be quick.

She spotted a book on one of the tables in the waiting room; on an impulse, she picked it up and took it with her when the nurse told her that Jasper was ready to see her.

Her hands were shaking. She glanced at a bathroom mirror as she walked by—she was as pale as a ghost. She'd only put on a little bit of lip gloss that morning. Her lips were almost the same color as her face.

She knocked on the frame of the Jasper's door.

"Come in."

He was in bed, still dressed in a hospital nightgown.

"Did you bring me more books?" he asked.

She held up the book in her hand and noticed, with horror, that it was an old Reader's Digest Condensed Books edition leading off with a Dick Francis novel. Dick Francis was a wonderful writer, but as a bookseller Angie could never have brought a condensed edition to *anyone* as a gift. Completely out of character.

Jasper reached for the book.

She had to say something, quick.

"How's your prognosis? Are you busting out of here anytime soon?"

"I should be fine to go in a few days," he said. "I'm fully hydrated, anyway, and that was the part they were most worried about."

"Hydrated?"

She still hadn't given him the book.

"Yes, it puts a strain on the heart. Along with all the caffeine I was taking."

"Oh, no," she said, putting the book down on a side table and taking his hand. "Was it the coffee from the bookstore?"

"No, no. Don't worry about that. If it wasn't all the NoDoz I was taking, it was the energy drinks. Or the stress."

"But what if—"

"Don't worry about it," he said firmly.

"Okay," she said. "I've been working on not taking too many burdens onto my own shoulders. I will *not* blame myself for your collapse from stress and too much caffeine."

"That's good," he said. "Now, please? The book? I'm desperate for something, *anything* to read."

She wished she had something clever to say that would prove him innocent or guilty in one witty line. But she didn't. Sighing, she handed over the book.

"It was a last-minute thing," she said. "I mean, I realize that—"

He smiled broadly at her. "I remember these! My grandmother had a hundred of 'em."

She winced.

"No, seriously. I love them! And it starts out with a Dick Francis novel, too…I haven't read that one. Thank you. You knew that I couldn't keep up with anything heavy right now, didn't you?"

She couldn't say a word. Not a single word.

Jasper Parris practically hugged the book to his chest. "Thank you," he repeated.

"You're welcome. I had no idea it would go over so well."

"Someday, when all of this is over, I'll paint you a scarf," he said. "What would you like on it?"

"Turner," she said. It hadn't been on her mind, exactly, but as soon as she said it, she knew it was the right thing to say. "Something by J.M.W. Turner. To remind me of Reed. That's how we met—over one of Turner's paintings."

"Turner," Jasper said. "That old curmudgeon. People like to say that he was a predecessor of the Impressionists, but I think he was just losing his eyesight and painting from memory, face pressed up against the canvas."

It was a harsh statement, and one that Angie hadn't expected.

"If you'd rather not—" she said.

"No, I'll do it. One in the style of Turner, and another one in the style of Monet. Then you can see what a real master looks like. Even on a scarf."

She smiled. "Thank you. That sounds even better. I'll wear the scarf when the painting is found."

"Oh? Are there any updates about the painting?" Jasper asked eagerly.

"Nothing yet," said Angie, "But I'll let you know."

"Thanks, and I won't forget about those scarves."

"Me neither," she said. She gave him a thumbs up and then hurried out of the room.

"Are you sure it was Jasper, Angie?" asked Aunt Margery?

Mickey and Angie had blustered into the bookstore to regroup after Angie's revelation. Aunt Margery had shushed them, and then she had corralled them into the back room to get away from the sharp-eared treasure hunters. Mickey was sitting on a table, dangling his legs and listening to Angie explain everything to Aunt Margery.

"Jasper is incredibly artistic. Have you seen those ties? Imagine what he could do with real paint and canvas. He keeps a low profile, and his family wasn't wealthy—it's possible he needed the money."

Aunt Margery nodded. "It's true. The Parris family wasn't wealthy, but they have been around the island for a long time. They do own some land though."

"I didn't know that. I thought Jasper rented the apartment down near the wharf. What land are you talking about?" Asked Angie.

"Over past the giant oak, they have a small cabin. Jasper goes there sometimes to think, paint, at least he used to when he was younger."

"Aunt Margery! Why didn't you tell me before?"

"Sweetheart, you never asked before, and until today, you didn't have a reason to."

"I'm going to check out this cabin while Jasper is still in the hospital. If there's evidence there, then I can tell detective Bailey, and we can finally find Reed's killer!"

"I'm going with you," said Mickey, in an authoritative tone that Angie almost didn't recognize.

"I'd tell you not to," said Aunt Margery, "but what good would that do?"

∽

The cabin was secluded, to say the least. They navigate a series of branching dirt roads and managed to get lost only once. Then they parked one the side of the great oak tree Aunt Margery had mentioned and walked from there. 100 yards down a small foot path, they spotted the cabin.

It was a small brown building that looked at least 100 years old. They didn't see any cars parked outside, nor was there any light from the windows, so they deemed it safe to investigate.

As Angie walked up to the cabin, she tripped on an exposed root and started to fall. Mickey swooped in and caught her. For a moment she was frozen in his embrace, peering up at at the charming face that she had come to take for granted. There was something impish about the way his eyes danced, and something deeply endearing about the laugh lines that were just beginning to show around his mouth and at the corners of his eyes. She had forgotten how to look at this face and see more than a friend, but she was remembering now.

And this was not the time for it.

At least Mickey seemed oblivious to her thoughts. "You okay?" he asked.

"Yeah, I'm fine." Perfectly fine. Blushing? Who was blushing? Not her.

He put her down and made his way to a cabin window. Right. They had come here for a purpose that had nothing to do with revisiting old feelings. She joined him at the window, and then drew in a quick breath.

"B-I-N-G-O," sang Mickey.

Angie agreed.

In the cabin was a small wooden table covered with paint brushes, painting knives, and a canvas. More tables containing paint tubes, additional canvases, and stacks of glossy paper bearing indistinct images lined the edges of the room. Above them, the walls were covered with printouts of the lost Monet. Arrows were drawn on each print to indicate important parts of the painting. The cabin looked like a forger's paradise. It wasn't quite a smoking gun, but it would give Detective Bailey a place to start, at least.

Angie pulled out her phone to call him, but there was no cell signal in this remote part of the island.

"Mickey, I want to take a closer look, do you think we can get inside?" said Angie.

"Yeah. Probably. Are you sure you want to?" as he asked he already knew the answer. He walked around the cabin and found a window that looked like it might be open.

"This window," he said, "Is too high for either of us, but I can probably put you on my shoulders and you can get in."

Angie smiled. "Okay, let's do it."

Mickey crouched down and she jumped on his back. After a little wobbling, they managed to steady themselves next to the window.

"Think you can get in there, Agatha?" as he asked he gave her legs a little squeeze to show he was joking.

"Sure, Baker," Angie teased. "What kind of code name is that, anyway?"

"An accurate one," Mickey chuckled. "Now stay focused. I'm not carrying you around for my health."

Angie's smile faded. Considering that he had just been discharged from the hospital, letting her climb all over him probably wasn't doing his health any favors. She turned her attention to the window and pushed it open. Then she climbed through it and half-jumped, half-fell into the cabin. She just barely landed on her feet.

She hurried to the door and unlocked it for Mickey.

"Wow. Look at this place," he said as he entered.

There were not only painting supplies all over the cabin, but little notes Jasper had made for himself about the different details of the lost Monet. The stacks of glossy paper turned out to be print-outs of other paintings, most of them by Monet. A clear plastic bag containing bundles of white silk ties occupied one corner of the floor, and in another, Angie saw... something.

"What's that?" she asked, pointing at the large, bright blue object she had just noticed on the floor.

They both bent down to inspect the object and knocked heads in the process.

Mickey hissed softly and rubbed his much-abused head. "Sorry, Angie," he said, and then his expression changed. Their faces were incredibly close, and for a moment, all they could do was look at each other. Mickey slowly reached out to touch her forehead where it had collided with his. An additional apology, or a gentle rebuke? Angie didn't know. She blinked once, then felt her cheeks heat. Again. Goddamn it. Then she thought of Walter, and quickly turned away.

"Sea glass," said Mickey, breaking the awkward silence, "I've never seen a chunk that big. And look here." He pointed to a rusty stain on the glass. "Either that's paint, or we've found the murder weapon. And it doesn't really look like paint."

"Mickey, I..." She stopped herself, not even sure what she was about to say. She had started her day afraid that he might be the murderer's second victim. Now she was breaking into private property with him and remembering the kind of mischief they used to get into in their teens. It must be her relief that made her feel so nostalgic, nothing more.

He smiled wryly at her, almost as if he could hear her thoughts. "You need to tell Detective Bailey," he reminded her. "Come on, let's go back to the car."

Chapter 17

THE LOST MONET

When the painting was finally found, it was anticlimactic for Angie. After she pointed Detective Bailey toward the cabin in the woods, and he found the bloodstained sea glass, it hadn't taken long for Jasper to be taken into custody. Gradually, the other details of Reed's murder were revealed. Amidst all the sensation of the solved crime, the discovery of the painting seemed comparatively insignificant.

It was December seventeenth, the anniversary of the letter from the mysterious lover promising that shat she would view the painting in secret. Locals and tourists alike gathered at the Whaling Museum to see the painting, which was now on public display for the first time.

Wyatt Gilmore stood in front of the crowd, wearing the biggest smile Angie had ever seen on his face. It made him look far younger and less jaded than usual. "I couldn't have done it without the help of several people who live here on Nantucket," he said. "I'd like to especially thank the staff at the Chamber of Commerce, who were so helpful throughout the search. Tabitha Crispin? You're my hero."

Everyone clapped politely, even though they all knew by then what wasn't being said: that Jasper Parris had *not* been helpful in finding the lost Monet painting.

In fact he'd been quite the opposite.

"And to Walter Snuock, thank you very much for providing us the opportunity to search for the painting. This has been one of the most interesting holiday seasons that I've ever had, to say the least."

More applause. Walter was standing behind Wyatt. He leaned forward and said into the microphone, "It has been my honor to sponsor the treasure hunt."

"And to the staff of Pastries and Page-Turners and the Nantucket Bakery," Wyatt said, "I couldn't have done it without you. Your assistance, research, and personal encouragement has meant the world to me. When I arrived here on Nantucket, I was at the end of my rope on a personal level. Thanks to you, I not only have found the Monet painting, but I've begun a new life in Boston with the HFC Investment Group, friends of Mickey Jerritt at the Nantucket Bakery. I cannot express the gratitude that I feel at this moment."

He had tears in his eyes as he looked around the room. And then, when he was sure that he had caught Angie's attention, he winked.

She smiled and winked back. She was glad Wyatt had found the painting. His investigations into land ownership had led him to the same location that the Beauchamps had found. Wyatt had gone to Sconset on his motorcycle and found the painting.

The Beauchamps had disappeared. They left Angie a nice note, taped to the back door of the café, thanking her for the coffee and the support. They promised to stay in touch, and offered her a place to stay if she ever decided to visit Boston.

Wyatt's speech went on, but she let her attention slide.

Jo was back on the island, and she now stood behind Mickey. Mickey's skull had proved to be more or less intact, but his twin sister still worried about him. People kept coming up to shake his hand and tell him how glad they were he had helped uncover Reed's murder. Mickey gave all the credit to Angie, but it was obvious that Mickey was touched. It was especially obvious because he was wearing his Santa-Claus suit again, although his hat was still hanging off the whale skeleton overhead.

Aunt Margery was sitting in a chair beside Mickey, surreptitiously reading a book on her phone as the speechmaker switched from Wyatt to Carol Brightwell. In the middle of the crowd, Janet sat with her parents, who had been shocked about the events that had apparently been going on right under their noses.

The big piece of sea glass had tested positive for human blood matching Reed's blood type. The forensics lab in Boston was going to run a DNA test on several hairs that had been caught in the surface of the worn glass, and they also had the clothing and shoes that Jasper had been wearing when Reed's body was found.

Angie had been wrong about Tabitha Crispin. She wasn't involved in the mystery, nor did she turn out to be related to the mysterious lover. The property records for the house in Sconset showed that the family who owned the house was the Snuocks. The mysterious lover had been none other than Eliza Churchill, née Snuock.

That made Walter the probable owner of the painting. He had said that if it *did* turn out to be legally his, then he would officially donate it to the island of Nantucket in perpetuity of something-or-other trust. The legalese made Angie's eyes glaze over. At any rate, a hunt for any heirs on the Churchill side was still ongoing.

Other people still had work to do. But from Angie's perspective? It was over. Well, almost over. She still had one last story to collect: Jasper's.

Detective Bailey had taken over the investigation and even thanked Angie for her help. That didn't stop him from asking the thousand and one methodical, inevitable details that he wanted in order to finish off the case, but Angie was happy to comply.

Jasper was in jail.

Once Detective Bailey had confronted Jasper with the evidence from the cabin, Jasper promised to admit to the murder and explain everything on one condition. He wanted his ex-wife and children in witness protection before he said a word.

Detective Bailey had agreed, and Jasper had told him everything, but he hadn't told Angie.

One last story.

∽

Angie went to visit Jasper in jail, bringing several books with her. Another Dick Francis book, a couple of Inspector Montalbanos, some Mary Stewarts and a Mrs. Pollifax, because why not? She hadn't had the stomach to bring him a romance. The books were still being processed and hadn't been given to him yet.

"Hi Jasper," she said to him. They sat at a plain-looking fold out table in a small room. There was a window where a guard watched their interaction, but it felt almost pleasant compared to the rooms she saw in the movies.

"Hi Angie," he said, "thanks for coming to see me."

"Well, detective Bailey said I should hear your side of the story."

"How did you first know it was me?"

She smiled faintly. "A picaso quote. You mentioned it when we spoke at the beginning of the treasure hunt. You said, good artists copy, great artists steal. I heard that again from one of my sources, and it made me think of you. Once I had information on how the world of forgery worked, it all started to add up."

"You know, I wanted to be an artist when I was growing up," he said with an answering smile and a hint of sadness in his eyes. "I made it to my second year of college and realized that I wasn't going to make it. Not only is the market for art terrible unless you're already famous and the beloved of some art movement or another, but I lacked that spark of creativity that every true artist needs. I had technique without originality, so all I was ever really good at was copying other artists."

He looked off into the distance over her head.

"I moved on with my life," he said finally. "I had some small victories, I earned admiration for my ties, and I got a position that allowed me to use my background in the arts for the greater good. I like to think that I did more good than harm in life. I had a few secret victories"—he smiled at her—"but it was a case of too little, too late, and I couldn't tell anyone anyway. Do you know who I sold the forged painting to?"

"I certainly have an idea."

"Someone in the Mafia."

"That's what I thought. But Jasper, why?"

"Truthfully, I was young, and stupid, and poor. I met some guys in the North End of Boston, and they knew I could paint, and then the whole thing just got out of hand. Once I sold it, I wasn't that worried. I never considered what would happen if the real painting was ever discovered. Then I got married, had kids, and I mostly forgot about this huge secret. But when Walter came up with the treasure hunt idea, I got worried. I promised myself I would do anything to protect the secret, and keep my family safe from the mafia."

"But why Reed? He was such a nice man."

"I don't think he suspected me before he got to the island. When we met, we immediately got into an argument about art. Turner versus Monet, as you know. He mentioned off-hand that he was hunting a forger, and was only registering for the treasure hunt so he could go snooping around. I almost lost it. I'm not sure if he knew right there that I was a forger, but I think he suspected."

Angie nodded, but couldn't bring her self to say anything.

"I followed him down to the beach. I didn't have a plan, but I was scared. Scared for my life, for my kids' lives. Angie, I know it doesn't make it better, but I didn't feel like I had a choice. If Reed exposed me as a forger, there's no telling what they would do. I saw the piece of sea glass on the beach, and fear just took over. I guess you know the rest."

Angie felt a range of emotions. Anger at Jasper for the murder of her friend. Grief for Reed who had died at the hands of this man. And also sorrow for Jasper, and his family, who had an uncertain future ahead of them.

"I don't expect to live long," he said cheerfully. "I have a bum ticker, and the mafia is likely after me. But I think my family will be safe, and that's what's important."

"Thanks for telling me. I see why Detective Bailey wanted me to speak with you," she said.

Jasper nodded.

"Good-bye, Jasper," said Angie as she walked out.

"Good-bye, Ms Prouty."

The forensic scientists in Boston reported that Reed's time of death had been close to six p.m., not eleven as the original examiner had guessed. Detective Bailey reported drily that there would probably be a training class coming out of this as punishment for the screw-up. Nobody liked training classes.

They also reported that Jasper's coffee hadn't been poisoned—a question that Detective Bailey had asked them long before Angie had thought of it. Reed's luggage was found eventually, and Reed's cell phone company was able to track his phone to somewhere out in the Atlantic. The current had carried it away.

Jeanette had been upset that the paperwork she had so painstakingly culled from Sheldon's files would come to nothing. At least, until Aunt Margery had asked to review it all as research for her next book, *The Lost Monet: The Island of Nantucket and the Painting that Time Almost Forgot*. Jeanette, assured that she would be mentioned in the book, immediately became her normal, cheerful self again.

Angie finally tried a fruitcake cupcake, but only because Jo literally shoved it into her face while Mickey watched, giggling helplessly. It *was* pretty good.

She finished the Louise Penny book while huddled in the back of the stock room for an hour. It was excellent, and she felt much better.

Then Detective Bailey called to say that the phone company had also gone through Reed's phone records and discovered...that he hadn't called or messaged anyone else on the island. There was no secret "special friend."

It had hit her hard. Reed Edgerton had been a solitary yet wonderful man. He shouldn't have had to die alone like that.

~

When she went to Reed's funeral in Cambridge, she realized that *alone* was not a word she could use to describe Reed any more. The funeral was, not to put a fine point on it, packed.

She sat in the middle of the throng, surrounded by people who had known him longer than she had.

They all seemed to know her, too.

"Angie Prouty? You're the bookseller from Nantucket, aren't you? Reed mentioned you! He said you were such excellent company at art shows!" And then a laugh. She must have heard the same things a dozen times at least, with multiple people all nodding at the same time. Reed's sister Heather had been one of the ones to say it the loudest.

His casket was surrounded by flowers and prints of his favorite paintings. She recognized Turner's slave ship painting, of course, and most of the others present. The one that had stood out to her, though, was a painting of a woman standing on a hill above the viewer, holding a parasol. It was a sunny day, and the wind had caught the ribbons of her bonnet, drawing them across her face. Behind her was a boy, looking less than enthused.

Woman with a Parasol – Madame Monet and Her Son, dated 1875. It was by Monet. How strangely appropriate.

She had brought with her a printout of the new painting—or rather the one that had been recently rediscovered—*Boats at Sunset, Saint-Adresse*. She had been shocked when she first saw it in person. It was so much more vibrant and alive than she had anticipated. It was a genuine pleasure just to look at it.

How anyone could have stood to keep it hidden for so long, she would never understand.

She tucked the printout in his casket.

Walter hadn't gone into the funeral with her—he had never met Reed in life, and felt like he'd be intruding—but he was waiting for her when she came back outside. He wrapped his arm around her and walked her back to his car. She might not know exactly where she stood with him, or what would happen to them in the coming months, but she was learning to live with a little uncertainty. And ironically, given recent events, she was gradually learning how to put her trust in others, and most importantly, in herself.

Christmas was just ahead, the bookstore was going to be busy. Honestly, she felt nothing but gratitude at the moment.

By the time they made it back to Nantucket, it had started to snow, and all the Christmas lights were twinkling in the dark.

I can do this, she told herself, and for once she wasn't just trying to reassure herself. *I can do this.* She and Walter were standing at the rail together, watching the island slide by. She lightly bumped shoulders with him in a companionable way, and he leaned down to kiss her.

"Merry Christmas," he said.

"Merry Christmas."

THANK YOU!

Thank you so much for reading Pride and Prejudice! Just like baking the perfect cake, the process of publishing this book required inspired prose chefs, delightful literary ingredients and lots of patience. It was not quite easy as pie but we feel that the final product really takes the cake. We hope you agree.

Books with reviews sell like hotcakes so we'd love it if you would be kind enough to take two minutes right now to leave a review of the book. To leave a review simply visit the **book page on Amazon** and click the button that says *Write a Customer Review*.

Pride and Prejudice is book 2 of the Angie Prouty Nantucket Mysteries, book 1 is available now! Get **Crime and Nourishment** from Amazon today.

Thank you for joining us on this adventure!

- The Team Behind Miranda Sweet

ABOUT THE AUTHOR

Miranda Sweet is a collaboration of authors, writers, editors, creatives, and cozy-mystery lovers. Miranda Sweet novels can be relied upon for classic cozy themes, settings and characters. Her books are best enjoyed with a hot beverage and a pastry.

To learn more about Miranda Sweet and get free books and recipes visit **MirandaSweet.com**

Made in the USA
Middletown, DE
30 December 2017